VISIONS OF RUIN

NP Novellas:

VISIONS OF RUIN

Mark West

NewCon Press
England

First published in the UK 2022 by
NewCon Press
41 Wheatsheaf Road,
Alconbury Weston,
Cambs, PE28 4LF

NPN017 (limited edition hardback)
NPN018 (paperback)

10 9 8 7 6 5 4 3 2 1

ISBN:

978-1-914953-14-9 (hardback)
978-1-914953-15-6 (paperback)

Cover layout and design by Ian Whates

Typesetting and editorial meddling by Ian Whates

Monday 26th August 1985:

Drove to Barton Point with Mum. She didn't say much and we listened to music for most of the journey, including the Hits 2 one she bought me for passing my "O" Levels. The camp is as bad as I expected but, like she said, at least it's free. Is it horrible that I'm not looking forward to this holiday at all?

One

"Here we are," said Mum as she turned off the coast road into a narrow lane, lined on both sides with bushes.

Sam pulled off his Walkman headphones as they passed under the grubby overhead sign for *The Good Times Holiday Camp*. As a welcome, it failed to suggest the place would try to live up to its name.

"It'll be fine," she said and switched off the car stereo, silencing The Bangles mid-song.

"Yes," he said, trying to re-assure her.

Mum smiled, put her hand on his leg and gave it a quick squeeze. "That's the spirit, Sammy."

The lane opened onto a roundabout. To the left were three buildings, all looking tired and well past their prime. The first had Reception/Shop above its glass doors while the second had a sweep of neon on the roof, which made the Starz Bar seem a little more glamorous but not by much. The third building, much smaller, was an arcade and a playpark stood in front of it, a handful of small kids enjoying the swings and slides.

A girl, watching them, stood by a sign that pointed away from the building, marked 'to the park'. She was about Sam's height, with dark hair cut into a bob, wearing a t-shirt and shorts. He thought she looked really pretty but she glanced at him and away without a second's consideration.

"Hey," said Mum, "at least there's someone else here your age."

"She's hardly going to want to hang around with me, is she?"

"Why not? You're cool and handsome."

"I know you have to say that because you're my mum, but you're wrong."

"You'll see," said Mum and steered the Chevette into one of the half dozen parking spaces in front of reception. She leaned her head against the back of the chair and blew out a breath, shifting some strands of her perm off her forehead. "Come on, let's go and get signed in. You can pretend you're not looking at the pretty girl by the sign."

"You're not funny, Mum."

"I live in hope that one day I will be," she said and got out.

The building was L-shaped, the shop to the left. The reception area was small, with two chairs that looked like the ones Grampy kept in his shed because "one day they'll be back in fashion" against the wall next to a rack of leaflets and pamphlets for local attractions. A counter bisected the room and, behind it, were a lot of pigeon holes. A window looked into an untidy office, where a woman sat at a desk with her back to them. Mum pressed the small bell on the counter and it made the woman in the office jump. She got up quickly and came through into reception.

Sam stared at her. If the girl by the sign was pretty, this woman was a knock-out. Somewhere in her early twenties, she wore a blouse with a lot of the buttons undone, her chestnut brown hair tumbling to her shoulders, feathered around her face.

"Bus coming," whispered Mum.

Sam shut his mouth quickly.

"Hi," said the young woman, "welcome to Good Times, my name's Jess. Can I help you?"

"I hope so, Jess," said Mum, in that irritating way she had of using a person's name when she didn't really know them. She'd told Sam it was a friendly thing to do but it made him cringe. Jess didn't seem to mind one way or the other. "We've got a caravan booked for the week."

"Excellent," said Jess and glanced at Sam quickly. He felt the heat rise in his cheeks and suddenly he was too hot and didn't know what to do with himself. "Just you and your son?"

"Yes, I'm Carol Parker and this is Sam."

"Pleased to meet you," said Jess politely, and she ran her finger down the ledger book on the counter. "Here we are," she said and unhooked a key from the pigeon holes. "You're in van 25. If you follow the road round the camp, you'll find it easily enough." She turned the ledger around and handed Mum a pen. "Just sign here."

Mum signed and Jess gave her the key.

"Thank you," Mum said.

"You're welcome," said Jess, with a smile that lit up her face.

Sam felt himself blush some more and just wanted to get out of the orbit of this woman before he exploded. He pushed open the door and held it for Mum.

The girl by the sign had gone and as Mum reversed out of her spot, Sam looked towards the caravans. The closest were big and reminded him of the Holimarine ones they'd stayed in before Dad left, but didn't look anywhere near as classy. Most were grubby and in need of paint and the grass around them was tufty, as if the gardener couldn't really be bothered.

Mum drove slowly along the road to avoid the little kids playing football or racing along on their bikes, none of them with an ounce of road sense. The caravans got smaller the further they went, until they were pretty much the size that could be easily towed behind cars.

To the left, beyond a thick hedge, were some fields that led up to a small wood. The sky glowered over the treetops, filled with grey cloud.

Mum turned off where an arrow indicated and pulled up beside one of the smaller vans. "Our home from home," she said. "What do you think?"

Sam stared at the caravan but couldn't hurt her feelings by telling the truth. "Looks all right," he lied. Moss grew around the upper edges of the windows and the frosted glass panel in the door had a crack with masking tape stuck over it. It might have been a four-berth, if they were lucky, but he wasn't going to bet on it.

"Of course it does," said Mum, her enthusiasm as false as his words. "I thought it'd be bigger though." She got out and opened the boot. Sam hefted out their suitcase before she could grab it. Instead, she picked up a rucksack. He followed her to the door and she went up the two steps, made of loose bricks and paving slabs that looked about ready to collapse. She unlocked the door, having to wiggle the key to do so, pushed it open and went in. Sam followed.

The caravan smelled of cleaning products and fried bacon. The kitchen was in front of them, the lounge to the left, cushioned seats around the walls surrounding a wooden table.

"That's the one that folds down into a double bed," said Mum.

To his right were three doors. The first was the bathroom and he peeked in, saw the sink, toilet and a shower stall. The door at the end opened onto a bedroom, almost filled by a double bed.

His room was narrow enough that it seemed an afterthought, with just enough space for a small chest of drawers and bunk beds. A window overlooked the road and field.

"Shit," he muttered to himself.

"What's the bed like?" Mum put her hands on his shoulders and leaned around him to peer into the room. "Oh," she said.

"It's fine, it's not a problem."

She rubbed his shoulders. "Yes it is, love. I didn't think to check. Listen, we can set up the table in the front and I'll sleep there and you can have the back bedroom."

He absolutely didn't want to sleep in bunk beds - they didn't even seem long enough for him – but he couldn't say that to Mum, not now. She'd pulled off a miracle even getting them this short holiday, how could he spoil everything before they'd even started? "No, I'll be…"

A knock at the door saved him. He and Mum looked at one another, then at the door and she went to answer it.

Sam sat on the lower bunk. The mattress sagged underneath him like soggy cardboard.

"Sam? It's for you."

"Me?" He got up and looked through the doorway.

Mum was smiling as she chatted with someone he couldn't see, though he could hear the female voice. Who could it possibly be? He felt his cheeks flare with heat. He only knew Jess. Why would she be here?

He stepped into the corridor and the girl who'd been standing by the sign looked up at him.

"This is Polly," said Mum. "Polly, this is Sam."

"Hey," said Polly. "I saw you and your mum drive in and thought I'd say hello."

"Isn't that nice?" asked Mum with a smile and dropped Sam a wink Polly couldn't see.

"Not really, Mrs Parker," Polly said. "I've been here a while and Sam's the first person I've seen the same age as me."

"Well, say something Sam," urged Mum.

What could he say? Why would this girl – this, admittedly, very pretty girl – be at the door of his caravan, wanting to speak to him? What the hell was going on? "Hi," he said.

She smiled, tilting her head to one side and Sam felt something ping in his belly. "Hey. Listen, I know you just got here and everything but I'm genuinely going insane because there's no one around to speak to. Did you want to go into Barton Point with me?" She looked at Mum now. "I mean, if you're okay with that, Mrs Parker?"

"Yes, of course." Mum took out her purse and gave Sam a fiver. "Go with Polly and treat yourself to a bag of chips or something."

Things seemed to be moving at light speed and Sam felt like he was being left behind. Why would a pretty girl want to go into town with him? "Shouldn't I help you unpack?"

"Don't be so silly, go off and have a great time." Mum almost pushed him out the door. "You take care, you two."

Polly led Sam on a zigzag path between the motley of caravans, heading towards reception.

"How old are you?" she asked.

"Sixteen."

"Me too. So where are you from?"

"Gaffney."

"Never heard of it."

"It's in the Midlands. Where are you from?"

"Nottingham."

Any potential replies drained from his brain. Some lads at school could chat to girls like it was the most natural thing in the world and he so wanted to be them, but whenever Sam saw a pretty girl, he basically forgot how to talk properly. Why couldn't he now, miles from home, re-invent himself somewhat, become as cool and sharp in reality as he was in his mind?

Polly looked at him, as if waiting for a response. In desperation, he thought about what Mum might ask. "So have you been down here long?"

"A few weeks. Dad's an ace mechanic and works for one of the stock car crews. He has a lady friend, who lives in town and so we come down every year. He often stays overnight with her which means I'm left on my tod."

"Oh." How was he supposed to respond to that? Even cool and sharp Sam in his brain was stumped.

"It's not bad, just bloody boring when there's no one else about. That's why I knocked on your door." She stopped and looked at him. "Just so you know, that's all it is. Don't get any funny ideas, all right?"

He nodded and felt a mixture of relief and frustration. "Okay."

"Good." She started walking again. "So what did you do that was so terrible you get to spend time here?"

"Nothing," Until the weekend, Sam didn't think they were going on holiday at all. Mum had told him, through most of the summer holidays, that she couldn't afford for them to go anywhere.

"And why come on a Monday, what's wrong with Saturday?"

"Nothing." He shrugged, feeling a bristle of annoyance at her questioning. "It was all a last minute thing, she got the van through a friend of a friend."

"Maybe someone dropped out at the last minute," Polly said then seemed to make the connection herself. "Oh..."

"No idea." He felt his cheeks flare with another type of embarrassment. He didn't want her to think they were poor. "Mum likes doing things on the spur of the moment," he said, hoping it sounded more convincing to her than it did to him.

She either picked up on his tone or didn't care. "She sounds cool. So did you see much of Barton Point?"

"Not really, I was listening to music. Mum's fallen in love with this new band called The Bangles, says it reminds her of music she listened to when she was my age, so I wasn't paying much attention."

"Well you're in for a treat," she said with heavy sarcasm. "The front starts about half a mile up the road, the town's a lot smaller than you'd imagine, there's a Pontins camp on the other side of town and the docks. And that's your lot."

"You sell it well."

That surprised a laugh out of her, which pleased him.

"Good to hear, I'm planning to do tourism in Sixth Form."

"A wise choice."

She stopped by the sign at the roundabout. "Did you fancy walking? Or," she smiled slyly, "did you fancy going in style?"

"In style, absolutely," he said, happy to play along.

"I like your thinking, Sam. Okay, follow me."

Jess was at the reception counter and waved as they went by. He waved back and noticed Polly bite her lip but didn't know what that meant.

The Starz Bar, this close, looked tatty, with paintwork peeling and the stars and other stickers pitted by the weather. A pile of cigarette ends had been brushed into the corner of one step.

"What's this place like?" he asked.

"Glossy, sexy, full of neon and smoke and people dancing. Imagine everything you've read about the greatest discos in London and New York and wherever else."

"Really?"

She laughed. "No, you idiot, of course not."

Offended, he kept walking and she touched his arm. "I'm not taking the piss, Sam, I wondered exactly the same thing but it's just like you think it will be. It's something out of the mid-seventies, with a sticky dancefloor and lights like a school disco and a DJ who probably got into music in the forties."

"Sounds like my kind of place."

She stared at him and it took her a moment to realise he was kidding. She tapped his arm again. "You're funny, Sam, I like that."

He felt warmth spread over his chest, pleased with her words. Maybe real Sam could be as cool as the Sam in his head.

They passed the Good Times Arcade, the open door letting out a blast of electronic noise mixed with kids laughing and walked around the building to a car park. There was a pile of rubbish – planks, bit of metalwork and old chairs – in one corner and a small corral filled with bins in the other. A hut stood next to the entrance barrier and a man in his early twenties sat in it, reading a copy of *Your Computer* magazine.

Behind the hut were five Surrey bikes: twin seaters with bright red with white canvas roofs.

"Hi, Max," Polly said as they walked across the car park.

The man looked up and smiled, eyes bright behind his thick rimmed glasses as he tucked the magazine behind him. "Hey," he said, stumbling over the 'h', "Polly. You okay?"

"Uh huh. This is Sam, he's staying at the camp."

"Hi, Sam," Max said, struggling through his stutter.

"Hi," said Sam.

"We're heading into town, can you lend me a bike?"

"I can't do that, Polly," Max said, stumbling over the 'P'. "You know I got into trouble before."

"I might have signed a bike out under the name Madonna," Polly said, sotto voce, to Sam and he laughed.

Max shook his head. "Wasn't funny, I got a real bollocking."

"I'm sorry, Max, I won't do it again. If you lend me the bike, we'll get it back and I won't write anything in the book? Deal?"

He looked at her the way a teenager might look at a pesky kid sister – you knew she was going to cause you trouble, but you couldn't help giving in. "Back by tonight, yeah?"

"Have I ever let you down, Max?"

Max tried to say "frequently" but gave up, waving her and Sam away.

"Thanks," she said and blew him a kiss. "Enjoy your afternoon."

"Yeah yeah."

Sam hadn't been on a Surrey bike in years but it didn't take him long to get used to it as they cycled along the coast road, past big houses that looked out to sea. A break in the clouds bathed the town in bright sunshine and, from a distance, it looked glorious.

They passed a small pier then a much longer one with a theatre at the end of it, billboards filled with names he vaguely recognised from TV gameshows. They rode by amusement arcades, a small funfair and a crazy golf pitch, the pavements filled with bored-looking parents shepherding excitable kids who embraced cheap cuddly toys as if they were the Crown Jewels.

Polly parked outside The Golden Nugget, got his fiver cashed and used 'her secret method' on the tuppenny falls machines to actually increase their stake. They played until they were hungry and it was only then Sam realised that it was dark outside, the colourful bulbs at the entrance painting the pavement in a rainbow.

Thanks to her method, there was enough money for cod and chips twice and they sat on a bench to eat their wrapped meals, watching the world go by and content in their silence.

By the time they'd finished – and downed a can of Coke they shared – twilight was fading to darkness. He checked his watch, saw it was almost nine o'clock. "What time do you need to be back?" he asked.

"I'm sixteen, not six," she said indignantly, "and if Dad comes back tonight, it'll be close to midnight. How about you?"

"I'm sixteen, not six," he said, trying to sound as indignant as she had.

It made her laugh. "Let's head back. We can always check out Starz, so you can see it's just like having Las Vegas on our doorstep."

He put the chippy paper in the bin as Polly manoeuvred the bike around and pushed it into the road. As they pedalled away from what was clearly the bright centre of Barton Point, he looked into the closed shops, watching the reflections of him and Polly as they scooted past.

A couple of hundred yards or so ahead, two men came out of a side street, laughing and staggering. One, overly tall and painfully thin, pushed his companion into the road. The second man, in a white Adidas tracksuit, stumbled but managed to keep to his feet. He weaved towards the white lines, making no attempt to get back on the path.

Sam felt a little spike of worry a moment before he realised Polly had stopped pedalling. "Are you okay?" he asked.

"Uh huh." She didn't look at him. "Just seeing what they do."

"I think they're just drunk."

14

"That's what I mean."

Thin man stopped outside a building and pointed at something, laughing loudly. He called Tracksuit over, gesturing at something in a lit window. Tracksuit laughed too and hit the window hard enough for Sam to hear the thump. He looked at Polly and wondered if they should just turn off the coast road, to keep out of the way.

"That's the Museum Of Marvels," she said quietly.

"What?"

"This old boy called Roy runs the place. It's full of weird stuff. I like it."

Tracksuit grabbed Thin man and shoved him into the window. The glass bowed, catching the light as Thin Man pushed his friend away.

"You fucking idiot," he yelled, "I could have fallen through and died."

"As if."

"What do you mean, 'as if'? That glass could have smashed and dropped on me and sliced me fucking head off."

"We could smash it anyway."

Polly braked the bike to a halt. Sam watched the two men, who were close enough now that if they rushed the bike Polly and Sam would have to run themselves.

Thin man looked around. "I saw a cone somewhere, we could use that."

"I'll kick it," said Tracksuit and did. The glass cracked with the second blow and a light came on in one of the first floor windows. Thin man kicked at the glass too.

"What do we do?" Sam asked.

"We have to help Roy, this isn't fair." She turned in her seat. "There's a phone box further back, one of us could run to that and call the police."

Before Sam could reply, the front door of the museum opened and a man wearing a cardigan and dark trousers stepped onto the pavement. He walked into the glow of a streetlight, which caught the wisps of grey hair floating around his head and Sam could see he was old, probably in his seventies. As old as Sam's Grampy, in other words and Sam would hate for his Grampy to get picked on by a couple of drunken louts.

"What do you think you're doing?" demanded the old man.

Tracksuit stepped back to the kerb, hands up. "Not me, guv," he said, laughing.

Thin man moved sideways, as if trying to get into the museum. "We just want to see your displays."

"Come on, lads," said the old man, "you're drunk. Just leave it."

"I ain't drunk," said Tracksuit.

"He ain't drunk," said Thin man.

"How dare you?" demanded Tracksuit and kicked at the window again.

"Hey, hey," said the old man, "don't break my window."

Polly slid out of the bike. Sam stepped out on his own side, his stomach cramping with fear and anger. If these idiots started a fight the old man wouldn't stand a chance and even if they called the police, they'd never get here in time.

"We don't like being told what to do," said Tracksuit, squaring up to the old man. He was a good few inches taller and a lot broader.

"What do we do?" Polly asked.

Sam had never really been in a fight before and these louts carried themselves like they knew exactly how to handle trouble. But he couldn't just walk away. If he did and heard tomorrow the old man had been badly beaten, he'd feel terrible.

Thin man kicked at the window again.

"Please," begged the old man, "I can't afford to fix it."

Tracksuit swung a punch that almost lifted the old man off the ground, his breath woofing out of him. He staggered back and dropped to his knees, bending until his forehead touched the pavement. His gasps for breath were almost drowned by the mocking laughter of Tracksuit. "Come on, Grandad, I've got more of those to give you."

16

Sam felt a flash of anger and then Polly stalked away from the bike. He rushed to catch up with her.

Thin man reached into the window and grabbed what looked like a doll. "What the fuck is this?" he asked then noticed Sam and Polly. "Hey," he said to Tracksuit, "looks like we've got some tourists."

Sam's heart beat hard against his chest, nerves twisting his stomach.

"Leave him alone," said Polly.

Thin man laughed. He threw the doll onto the ground and rubbed his hands on his trousers.

Tracksuit laughed too. "Or what?"

"He's an old man," Polly said. "Just leave him alone."

Tracksuit glanced at Thin man. "Got a right one here," he said, then looked at Sam, who felt like he was about to fall into an abyss. "You want to keep your bird in line, mate."

"He didn't do anything to hurt you," said Sam, desperation clogging his voice.

"He stopped our fun," said Tracksuit and kicked at the old man, the blow glancing off his thigh.

Sam felt anger push past his fear. "Leave him alone."

"Or what?" Tracksuit repeated, lining up for another kick.

Polly rushed forward, grabbed his arm and yanked back. Off balance, Tracksuit swung for her but missed and she pushed him hard. He landed heavily on the pavement with a grunt.

Thin man went for Polly, his fist raised, but Sam got to him first, shoving him out of the way. Thin man spun on his heel, punching Sam's shoulder and instantly deadening his arm. Sam fell against the door of the museum, rattling the glass, his shoulder throbbing. He couldn't catch his breath, his lungs apparently shrunk.

Thin man grinned and pulled Sam away from the door by his jacket. "Stupid kid," he said, his breath stinking of old meat. "Now the grown ups are going to have to sort you out."

He drew his fist back and Sam reached for it. Thin man pushed him away and Sam's feet slid out from under him. Landing flat, wind knocked out of him, his head whiplashed against the pavement.

His field of vision went negative before bulbs of red burst across the sky, the sound of heavy fireworks filling his ears. He heard his heartbeat and a scuffle and someone shouted.

His vision went dark.

TWO

Sam felt a hand on his shoulder and slowly opened his eyes. The sky was dark and the girl looking at him, concerned etched on her face, was partly in shadow from the street-light.

"Polly?" Images rushed at him, of Thin man and Tracksuit and he pushed himself up onto his elbows. Blinding pain flared across his skull and he thought, for a moment, he was going to throw up.

"Take it easy, Sam," Polly said.

His throat felt dry but he daren't cough. "What happened?"

"You fell and hit your head."

He moved carefully and this time it didn't make him feel sick. "What about those men?"

"The one I knocked over didn't get up and I hit the skinny one with a traffic cone." She smiled. "Roy chased them off."

Another face came into view, the man's wrinkles deepened by the shadows. "I'm Roy," he said, "and you need to be careful, son, you've had a busy night."

"I'm okay."

"I'm not so sure.."

"Are you okay?" Sam asked.

"I'm fine." Roy smiled. "I've worked at the seaside all my life and wasn't always an old man."

Sam heard a clatter and glanced over Roy's shoulder. Tracksuit was struggling to get Thin man to his feet but finally managed it and they staggered away, holding onto shop fronts for support.

"How do you feel?" Polly asked.

"Like a brass band is playing inside my brain." Sam looked at their concerned faces. "You can't hear music too, can you?"

"No," said Roy. "I think I should take you to casualty."

19

"I'm fine," Sam insisted. It wasn't the first time he'd bumped his head and he was sure it wouldn't be the last. Besides, the last thing Mum needed now was getting a call to meet him at the nearest hospital. "Honestly."

Polly glanced at Roy. "I don't believe him."

"Me neither." Roy faced Sam. "I'm worried you might be concussed."

Sam looked at him intently, wondering if he was serious. He'd only bumped his head. "I don't have concussion. I'm pretty sure I wouldn't be conscious."

"That's not how it works," said Roy.

"Honestly, I feel okay." "I'm not sure," said Polly, "but I can get him home, we've got the bike to get us back to the camp."

"You're not going to change your mind, son, are you?"

"Nope," said Sam. "Sorry."

"Then in that case, I need to thank you both for helping me."

"It was nothing," Polly said but he cut her off, holding up his finger for silence.

"It really was," Roy corrected her with a smile. "You could have walked on by, Polly, but you didn't." He held out his hand to Sam. "I'm Roy Denman, thank you for helping protect me and my museum."

"I'm Sam Cooper," he said, shaking Roy's hand.

They pulled Sam slowly to his feet. A wave of dizziness coursed through him and he closed his eyes against it, head down until the awful sensation passed. Worried, Sam gently touched the back of his head, hoping against hope he didn't feel any blood in his hair. There was nothing and he breathed a sigh of relief.

"I really think I should take you to casualty."

"It's okay, Mr Denman," Sam said. He opened his eyes, the dizziness fading.

"Do you need us to help you sort out your window?" Polly asked. "You can't leave the museum like that."

"Polly, my dear," he said, putting his hand gently over hers, "if I can't get people into my museum during the day, they're hardly going to be rushing to come in at night, are they?"

With promises to let Roy know they were both okay, Polly and Sam walked back to the bike.

"Do you really feel fine?"

"Yes," Sam said, even though it felt like someone was tapping his temples with a metal tent peg. What if he did have a concussion? He'd read about them before, mainly headbangers going to too many Motorhead gigs, but he'd never known anyone who'd suffered.

"I don't believe you."

"You don't have to."

Clouds marred the night sky as they cycled back along the coast road. A car passed and the driver shouted "you haven't got any lights, you stupid kids," out his window.

Finally, they turned off into the lane and Polly huffed out a breath with relief. "Well, that ended up scarier than I'd thought it would."

"Same here."

"Thanks for grabbing that bloke and helping me," she said and offered him a shy smile. "Nobody's ever done anything like that before."

"It was nothing."

"Yes it was," she said and leaned over, kissing his cheek quickly. "Not that I'm saying you're my hero, or anything."

"Oh I understand." He caught her fleeting smile before she looked away. "And thanks to you too, nobody's ever hit anyone with a traffic cone for me before."

Polly steered them around the back of reception. The car park barrier was down and Sam slid out his side of the bike. His vision shifted like a badly tuned TV image and he pressed fingers to his forehead until the sensation passed.

"You all right?" Polly called.

"Fine."

He hefted the barrier up until Polly had ridden through then let it fall. She parked next to the hut Max had been sitting in.

"I told him I'd bring it back safe and sound."

They walked around the now dark arcade. Lights were on in the Starz Bar and Sam could hear a band playing very badly.

"Monday's never a good night for the club," said Polly, as if that explained everything and stopped on the edge of the roundabout. "Sorry about your head, Rocky, didn't mean to get you into a fight."

"It wasn't your fault."

"Well, it kind of was. I did wade in."

"We couldn't let them get the better of Roy."

"Not at all. He's nice and his museum is ace, some of the stuff in it is really weird. We could go over tomorrow."

Her words made him feel brighter. "You want to hang around tomorrow?"

She stopped. "Why wouldn't we?"

"Well," he said, struggling for words, "I didn't…"

Polly held up her hand. "Don't get any funny ideas, okay, this is just as friends."

"Yes," he murmured, chastened at the speed she'd shot him down.

"Did you have anything planned with your mum tomorrow?"

"No idea."

"I'll call for you, we'll sort it out."

"Did you want me to walk you back?"

She gave him a big smile. "Uh uh, you just want to know where I live."

He returned her smile. "Caught me."

"Yeah, thought so." She tapped his shoulder playfully. "See you tomorrow, Romeo."

He waited until she'd disappeared into the block of larger caravans then followed the road around the edge of the camp. Street lamps stood at the edge of each block, giving enough light to see where he was going. Most of the vans were dark.

He walked slowly, his head still throbbing though the pain was much less sharp than it had been.

The large bush separating the park from the field and woods looked black and when something moved in it, the sound startled him. He paused, heard the squeak of an animal then all was quiet. Off to his right, a baby started crying in a caravan, the sound muted. A moment or so later, he heard an adult voice make soft cooing noises.

He walked on. The light at the end of the road flickered for a moment, drawing his attention. As he watched it, he heard something creak. It sounded like rope against a tree bark, as if someone had set up some kind of swing in the woods. The light clicked off as a breeze blew, rattling the bush and the trees beyond, leaves and boughs whispering.

The light flickered back into life and in the stuttering glow he saw the dark shape of a person. They seemed to be off the ground, feet dangling. The creaking sound got louder and made his head throb. Stepping back, heart racing, Sam tried to rationalise what he was seeing. Was it someone or the shadow of someone? He turned around but the road was empty and he couldn't see anyone in the gaps between the caravans either.

The creaking sound settled.

The light flickered quickly, the shape moving with the staccato movements of a flipbook and then it disappeared as the light failed.

One more creak then the sound of something heavy hitting the ground.

The light blinked back on. There was nothing on the ground and no dark shape hanging.

Blood thudding in his ears, Sam backed away, trying not to look at the light in case it flickered again, but he couldn't tear his eyes away. He went to his right, between two caravans, and walked further into the block, away from the road.

He changed direction, walking into the deep shadow between a caravan and a car. He could smell something sweet and his head ached. He wondered if he was lost.

A shoe scuffed on gravel and he froze, trying to place the sound. Footsteps, off to his right. Keeping close to the caravan, he made his way around it and saw someone walking towards him with a brisk pace.

He waited.

Mum, her dark curly hair bouncing with each step, walked into a cone of light and, without thinking, he stepped forward.

She started and pushed her hand hard to her mouth, as if to squash a scream.

"It's me," he said, feeling terrible for scaring her, "I'm sorry."

"Sammy?" She shook her head and put her a hand on her chest. "What're you doing, creeping around the caravans?"

"I was coming back and thought I saw someone."

"It was me, you nitwit. Bloody hell, Sam, you scared the living daylights out of me."

"Oi," came a muffled voice from inside one of the caravans, "people are trying to sleep in here."

Putting her finger to her lips, Mum beckoned him over and when he was close enough, she swatted his arm. "You really scared me."

"I'm sorry. Where have you been?"

"Frank called round, took me for a drink in the Starz Bar."

"Who's Frank?"

"The friend of a friend, it's his caravan."

"Is he nice?"

Mum held her hand flat and rocked it from side to side. "Enough about me, who did you see that freaked you out?"

"I don't know, I could just see their outline."

"Probably someone coming home from the club. I hope you didn't scare them."

"I hope I did, because they scared me."

24

Mum laughed, softly. "My gallant hero," she said and took his arm. "Well, you can escort me back and tell me all about your evening with the lovely Polly."

By the time they got back to their caravan, Mum knew as much as he would ever tell her about the time he'd spent with Polly. He didn't say a word about Roy, the thugs, the museum or him cracking his head. He thought it was for the best.

Three

Tuesday 27th August 1985:

It felt like someone was pressing down on Sam's forehead with a concrete block. He groaned but the vibration of sound made him feel nauseous so he stopped.

Something drummed above him and a gull dancing on the roof shrieked.

Sam slowly opened his eyes. The bedroom curtains were closed but thin enough to be almost worthless.

He rubbed his temples gently until the pain slowly shifted towards the back of his skull, as if to bury it in the pillow. After a minute or so, he sat up slowly, the nausea fading as he swung his legs off the bed, sitting with his hands on his knees.

He'd only felt like this once before, when he'd got drunk on White Lightning at a house party he went to with Andy, waking up with the sensation that everything in his head was either dead or fading fast.

But he hadn't drunk last night. He remembered the chips and arcades and making money then helping Roy at the museum and... He'd fallen. He touched the back of his head gingerly and there was a small stab of pain that made him wince.

Taking a deep breath, he stood up slowly, holding the upper bunk for support. The world swam briefly and he took a moment, until he felt confident he could walk without collapsing or being sick.

A door clicked and he heard Mum's feet on the lino. When she flopped down on a chair in the lounge, he felt the vibration of it through the crappy old caravan floor.

Once he was confident he could move without looking like a zombie, he walked carefully to the toilet.

He felt better after he'd showered and got dressed. The pain was down to a dull throb and some of Mum's paracetomol would shift it, though he'd nick them rather than ask, because she'd worry and the last thing he wanted to do on this holiday was cause her to fret. He didn't know what concussion felt like but he was pretty sure he didn't have it and he hadn't found any blood in his hair or coming out of his ears.

Mum sat at the table in the lounge, reading. A cup of coffee, almost drunk, sat next to an opened packet of cigarettes. Through the window he saw a sky full of dark grey clouds.

"Hey, Sammy," she said, resting her chin in her palm and giving him a lazy smile, "how're you feeling today?"

"Okay, you?"

"Didn't sleep so well." She paused and wrinkled her nose, fiddling with the packet of cigarettes. "You know," she said, watching her hands, as if he'd understand. "Plus it's overcast, which is very British seaside of the weather, isn't it?"

Sam glanced into the kitchen, saw the draining board was empty. "Did you want some toast?" he asked. She didn't eat much any more, seeming to exist mostly on coffee and cigarettes since the divorce. "That'll make you feel better."

"That sound lovely, Sammy, thank you."

The rain started while Mum had her shower. He watched *The Red Hand Gang* on the portable telly that was so old it had a tuning dial to find different stations and even then he couldn't get a decent picture, however much he adjusted the circular aerial.

"Watching anything good?" she asked, coming into the lounge, tucking her polo-neck into her jeans as she did.

"Nope."

"Did you want to come into town with me? We need some bits and pieces but I don't want to pay the prices in the camp shop."

"It's chucking it down," he protested.

"Our cagoules are in the car."

"We could take the car."

"How far is it to town?"

"Miles," he said with a grin.

"Miles?"

"It'll take hours."

"Okay," she said, returning his smile, "we'll take the car."

They put their shoes on and droplets of rain blew into the caravan when Sam opened the door. Mum put her handbag on top of her head and rushed out to the car, jogging on the spot as she tried to get the key in the lock, then jumped in and opened the passenger door. Sam locked the door and felt the rain soak into his t-shirt before he got in.

"I told you we'd have a good time with the English summer," Mum said.

"You're weird."

She drove slowly round to reception. A lone figure, hunched into a too-big cagoule, was walking down the lane. Mum slowed to pass them and Polly looked into the car, holding the hood of her cagoule in place. Her fringe was plastered to her forehead.

"Wind your window down," Mum said and Sam did. "Polly! Did you want a lift somewhere?"

"No thanks, Mrs Parker, I just wanted to get out of the van for a bit."

"But it's chucking it down."

"She's probably realised that," muttered Sam.

"Yes, I noticed," said Polly and Sam admired her ability to look as sincere as she sounded. "I just wanted to get some air, that's all."

"Okay," said Mum. "Actually, I'm glad I've seen you. Is there a little Co-op or something like it in town?"

"Yes, one street back from the coast road by the old pier."

"Thanks. And if you haven't got anything planned later, why not call in? I found some board games in the caravan, if you're interested. I mean, I know it's probably not cool or anything but we won't do much this afternoon if this rain keeps up."

Polly stuck up her thumb. "Thank you, Mrs Parker, I will." She gave Sam a little wave.

With a slight pang of embarrassment, Sam returned the gesture as Mum drove off. He quickly wound up the window.

"You could have asked her yourself," Mum said.

"I don't want to ask her on a date."

"Playing Monopoly is hardly a date, Sammy."

"No, it's not cool though either, is it?"

Mum laughed and pushed her Bangles tape into the stereo. "I grew up in the Sixties, kid, you have no idea what cool is."

The dark clouds merged with the sea, almost making the horizon invisible. People walked along the beach, sweeping metal detectors back and forth and a lone jogger came by, gaudy tracksuit glistening wet, their Walkman bouncing.

"That must be the old pier," Mum said.

It was the smaller structure Sam saw yesterday, made of wood and metal. Barely reaching the sea, it didn't have enough room for amusements or a café, just a handful of empty benches and an air of neglect. It looked, he thought, like it might fall over if there was a strong enough gust of wind. The proper pier, half a mile further along the prom, looked magnificent by comparison.

Mum turned into a street that, apart from an amusement arcade on the corner, could have been in Gaffney. They passed a secondhand bookshop, a clothes shop, an estate agents, a hardware store and a Spinadisc record shop.

At the next junction, she pulled up at the kerb even though the Co-op was a couple of hundred yards away. "I know you'd rather go into a record or bookshop than the Co-op so why don't you have a wander, I'll get what we need then come and find you."

"Are you sure?"

"Yes, just be ready. If I've got fridge stuff, I don't want to spend ten minutes trying to drag you out of the bookshop because you've found a Stephen King novel you don't own."

"Thanks, Mum."

The rain had settled into a drizzle as he walked, looking out towards the old pier. He decided to have a closer look and crossed the road. A pay telescope stood at the far end, drooping with disinterest now, and gulls hungrily circled a couple of bins. He leaned on the railing, facing towards the camp. The beach sloped down from the pavement and a woman sat on the sand next to one of the pilings.

She wore a baggy top, culottes and a straw boater, her blonde hair loose and seemingly dry. Looking towards the end of the pier, she craned her neck as if searching for someone, her shoulder moving slightly as if she was laughing or crying. He couldn't hear her doing either.

A light breeze blew up, bringing with it the crisp smell of damp sand and something else, a vaguely unpleasant scent he almost recognised. Rubbing his nose and feeling that something was out of place, Sam went back across the road to the bookshop.

He found a horror anthology he'd been searching for, the gaudy cover promising all manner of gruesome content, and got to the Co-op just as Mum came out. They drove back and she sang along to The Bangles. He carried the shopping into the caravan and Mum put it away.

"Bugger."

"What?" he asked, scanning the contents page to try and decide which story to start with.

"I forget to get cereal. Can you nip to the shop for me?"

"Really?" He held up the book, thumb at his place, as if that might make her realise how big a sacrifice she was expecting him to make. She gave him a look and he got up. "Okay."

"Thanks, Sammy, my purse is on the side."

He put his cagoule and trainers back on and went out into the drizzle, taking a wandering path towards reception. The rain had kept a lot of people in their caravans, adults talking while kids watched TV or played with toys. In one, a small boy sat snuggled into his dad as they read a picture book.

"Hey, Sam, where're you off to?"

Polly came from behind a caravan and when she smiled he felt something tickle through his chest.

"The shop, Mum forgot the cereal."

"Oh. Can I come with you?"

"It's not going to be very exciting."

"I know, but you and your mum are the first people I've spoken to today." She said it matter-of-fact, no sadness in her voice and it would be a long time before he fully appreciated what she'd said.

"I feel bad for you," he said and she laughed, falling into step with him. He liked the sound of her laugh, as though she'd been told a dirty joke and couldn't wait to pass it on.

"Did you check out Spinadisc? I love it in there, they have stuff I can't even find at home." She lifted her cagoule. A Bush personal stereo was clipped to the waistband of her jeans, the headphones hanging out of her pocket. "I love music."

"Me too."

They compared mixtapes they'd created from Top Of The Pops as they crossed the roundabout and went into the reception. A blonde woman, wearing red jeans and a white t-shirt, was sitting in one of the chairs by the door. Jess came through from the back office and smiled when she saw them.

"Hey Polly, nice to see you. And Sam, isn't it?"

The fact she remembered made him smile. Polly was pretty, no doubt about that, but in a cute Sarah Green from Blue Peter kind of way, while Jess was more movie star pretty, like Kathleen Turner. Gorgeous pretty. Out of his league pretty.

"Hey Jess," he said, hoping he sounded cool and older and someone she might be interested in even though, to his ears, he actually sounded younger than he was, his voice too high and crackly. He felt himself blush. "I just need something from the shop."

"Don't let her stop you," muttered Polly.

He glared at her, she smiled sweetly at him then went to the counter and started talking to Jess. Sam went into the shop, cursing his apparently complete lack of ability to talk to pretty girls. Why was it just him that suffered?

He quickly found the cereals and picked up a box of Cornflakes. So he wouldn't have to show Mum's purse, he took a pound coin out and went back into reception. The blonde woman hadn't moved and didn't even glance at him as he came in, her attention fixed on the counter area. Was she staring at Polly or Jess?

He walked across her line of vision, put the Cornflakes on the counter and Jess rang them up without saying anything. He paid and she gave him his change.

"So you're coming over tonight, Polly?" Jess asked.

"Yes, of course."

"Excellent." Jess looked at Sam. "Can I tempt you to the Tuesday Night Club?"

"What's that?"

"Tuesday's are normally dead," she said, "but we have the beer and drink delivery so it's busy for the staff. To blow off steam, we get together in the car park to have a drink and mess about."

"It's good fun," said Polly.

He was being invited to a party, by an attractive woman. This never happened. "Love to."

"Great," said Jess, "see you there."

Clutching his Cornflakes, Sam followed Polly out of the reception and as they crossed the roundabout she looked at him almost dismissively.

"What's the matter?"

"She's got a boyfriend, you know."

Was he that obvious? "I wasn't looking at her."

"Yes you were and her boyfriend is older, so I wouldn't bother."

"I didn't say I was going to bother, Polly. I didn't say anything at all."

"You didn't have to," she said and led the way to his caravan.

Four

The afternoon went quickly and the game of Monopoly proved Polly to be a shrewd player who gave Mum a run for her money. They listened to music – Polly had little speakers to plug into her walkman – and Mum cooked them all a couple of large Co-op pizzas to share.

It was a little after eight when Polly said they should be going and Mum shooed them out, telling them to have a good time.

It had stopped raining, the sky patchy with cloud, the day fading quickly enough some of the street light were on already.

"I like your mum."

"Thanks, she's all right. I think she enjoyed spending time with you."

"Why wouldn't she?" Polly said with a shrug.

In the car park, the industrial bins near the corner of the reception hid what seemed to be a sunken patio. Ratty deck chairs had been set out along with some electric lamps and a battered silver Boom Box played an old disco song he recognised because it made Mum dance every time she heard it.

Jess saw them and jumped up, waving. Sam felt his chest tighten as he took in her smile and waved back.

"Good to see you both," she said, "come on down."

He followed Polly down some concrete steps. Max, smiling shyly, sat near a girl wearing an oversized Frankie t-shirt, her perm peroxide blonde.

"Everybody, this is Sam." Jess pointed at the blonde. "That's Annie." The girl raised her hand and mouthed "hello".

Two lads, wearing jeans shorts and vests like they'd just escaped from a Wham video, leaned against the wall. "That's Phil," Jess said, pointing to the blond one, "and he's..." Sam didn't catch whether the brown haired lad was called Jim or Tim.

The group greeted Polly like an old friend.

"Drink?" Max asked her. He had a hand towel on his lap. When Polly nodded, he handed her a can of Woodpecker. "Not much choice, sorry." He looked at Sam. "What about you, mate?" It took him a while to get mate out and he had to wipe his mouth.

"Cider's fine," said Sam, not wanting to put Max on the spot.

"Good," said Max and tossed him a can.

"It doesn't seem that exciting," Jess said, leaning close enough to share the confidence their shoulders touched, "but it beats Tuesday night in the Starz." He felt slightly giddy at their proximity and could smell her perfume. "Gets a bit boring here sometimes."

She didn't need to apologise, he thought, all this seemed ridiculously exciting. Going to a party with people in their early twenties, drinking and listening to music was already cool, having the gorgeous Jess lean against him made it even better.

"It's fine."

Polly handed him a folded deck chair as Jess sat between Max and Annie. Polly snapped open her chair and sat across from them, Sam opened his and set it down beside Polly. She held up her can.

"Cheers," she said.

"Cheers," he said and they tapped cans.

The group proved to be a friendly enough bunch, drawing Sam into conversations he couldn't really follow. Polly threw herself into the mix and he admired her self-confidence. As the alcohol loosened them up, people began to sing along to the music. Annie launched into Laura Branigan's *Gloria* and had a remarkable voice.

"She sounds great," said Polly.

Jess leaned forward, the neckline of her t-shirt drooping enough that Sam couldn't resist looking. She touched a hand to the material, pushing it against her chest and he felt embarrassed that she'd caught him. "Annie works in the arcade and she's also one of the acts in the bar at night. She's off singing on the cruise ships next year."

Max stood up, swayed on his feet and sat down again. One of the lads laughed at him and he joined in, struggling to stand up. When he finally did, he planted both feet.

"It's time," he said and Annie groaned. "It's okay," he said, "it's not your turn."

"Why don't we send the new boy?" asked Phil, his bleached blond hair catching the light as he stood up.

Sam felt a quick charge run up his arms. Were they picking on him? Where was he going to be sent?

"That's hardly fair," said Jess.

"All's fair at Roof Race time," said Phil and gestured for his mate to get up.

"But it's my turn," Jess said and stood up, shaking out her hands. "I'm ready."

"Ready for what?" asked Sam.

"Roof Running," she said. "We time ourselves and at the end of the season, the fastest wins a prize."

"Been doing it for years," said Annie and her friends nodded in agreement. "Not too many broken bones, either."

Jess pulled Sam to his feet, her hands wonderfully smooth and cool and put her arm over his shoulder. "We climb up on the roof of the arcade, run across the bar and over the reception." She turned slightly. "Across the height restriction bar, down that stack of crates that look incredibly like steps and you're done. Quickest time wins."

"And you do this every week?"

"Yep," said Annie.

"I've never done it," said Polly and looked hurt she hadn't been asked. "What's the quickest time?"

"Thirty-two seconds," said Jim or Tim, looking pleased with himself.

Sam looked at the route Jess had pointed out, enjoying the feel of her skin against his neck.

"So what do you think, new boy?" asked Phil. "Think you could do it?"

Aware they were all looking at him, Sam knew the race sounded stupid and dangerous but he could be whoever he wanted to here, they didn't know him. And with Jess standing so close, her arm over his neck, he wanted to be the kind of teenager who said "right, fuck it" and did the dare. "Why not?"

Jess stepped away from him. "Nice move, Sam, I like your style."

"Kid's got balls," said Max, stumbling through 'balls'.

"Are you mad?" asked Polly. "What if you slip and fall?"

"I won't," Sam said, adrenaline pushing down the fear. He wouldn't fall. The others did it all the time, why should he be the exception?

"I'll go with you," Jess said. "We'll do it together and you can follow me so you know the best route."

Once up on the arcade roof, looking at several big puddles across it, Sam's doubts outweighed his adrenaline-fuelled confidence. The bar and reception roofs were peaked – what if his trainers slid on the wet tiles? That'd end this adventure real quick, wouldn't it?

Phil and Jim or Tim boosted him up and then gave Jess a lift. Sam helped pull her up. He noticed she was wearing loafers, which would give less grip than his trainers, suggesting you probably didn't need to be Spider Man to pull this off.

"So, here we are," she said and stuck out her lip to blow her fringe off her forehead.

The lights of Barton Point glittered to his right while ahead, the camp faded into the darkness of the wood beyond it.

"Ready?" called Phil.

Sam looked down at the expectant faces. By the barrier, the woman he'd seen earlier in reception was standing on her own, arms folded, looking up at the roof but not at him, her gaze fixed on Jess. Maybe she was a manager or something?

"Ready?" Jess asked him.

"Thirty two seconds, yes?"

She stuck up her thumb then leaned over the edge of the roof. "We're ready." To Sam, she said, "Just follow me. It's safe, we'll be fine."

"I'm not scared."

"Didn't say you were."

"Right," called Jim or Tim and held up his watch.

"Three," called Phil, "two, one."

"Go," they all shouted and Jess grabbed his arm.

They ran over the arcade, dodging the puddles as best they could. She jumped onto the Starz Bar and scrambled to the peak which was a flat panel, perhaps a foot or so wide. He followed her and the group roared them on but he daren't look down in case it threw his balance.

The reception roof had a similar panel and Jess took the corner of the L shape without slowing. The group clapped and cheered them on.

The height barrier was just ahead, much wider along the top from this angle than it had appeared from the ground. There was a slight gap between it and the edge of the roof.

"How do we get over?"

"Jump," Jess shouted over her shoulder, clearly excited as she slowed down, dropping to sit on the panel. She slid down the tiles and he followed. At the last moment, just before she kicked the gutter, she pressed her foot against a line of bricks that looked so out of place they might have been placed there for just this purpose.

She pushed and propelled herself onto the height bar.

Running on adrenaline and excitement, Sam followed and, for a moment, he was flying. Weightless.

Jess landed, the barrier wobbling a little. Sam, thinking for one awful moment he was going to miss and fall headfirst to the concrete, landed behind her. It wobbled enough to make him throw his arms out for balance, but he stayed upright.

"Shit," he said, heart racing.

Jess glanced over her shoulder, smiled and then somehow her feet got tangled together and she fell forward. Someone shouted. She threw out a hand and Sam grabbed for it, catching her wrist. Her momentum carried her over the edge of the barrier and, hanging in space, she clung to him in terror. Her weight shifted, twisting her sideways and then she was falling.

He braced his legs and then, suddenly, they weren't on the bar any more and he was looking at her and seeing railway lines behind her head.

"Sam!" she shouted.

The Jess he saw stared with wide, terrified eyes at something, or someone, just over his shoulder. He glanced, saw a man with a moustache and brown hair. He shouted, reached past Sam.

Sam heard the train. It sounded painfully close, the roar of its engine and wheels vibrating in his bones.

Jess hung in space, his grip the only thing stopping her falling. She wore a flower print summer dress, her arms glowing with a tan. He reached for her with his other hand but it wasn't his that he saw. The train horn went off, almost deafening him and he knew, if he looked over, he'd see the front of the engine, impossibly big, impossibly close.

She screamed.

Sam pulled back as hard as he could but didn't have any leverage. Jess screamed again, the sound ricocheting through his head as her sweat-slicked hand slipped through his.

He felt the air displaced by the train.

Their fingers slid apart and she fell.

The engine came into vision, shockingly fast and then she was gone in a red mist.

Five

Jess fell, screaming, but the others were below her now, Phil and Annie and Polly and Jim or Tim. They caught her, collapsing in a heap with the momentum.

Sam sat heavily on the edge of the height bar, watching them untangle themselves. Annie helped a trembling Jess to her feet.

"You coming down?" asked Phil, gazing up at him.

Sam let himself slip off the edge. Someone grabbed his legs, supporting him as he lowered himself down then let go, so he could drop the last few feet.

Max patted him hard on the shoulder.

"Nice one, mate," Jim or Tim said and punched the top of his arm.

Polly stood next to him. "You saved her."

"I don't know what I did," Sam said, his mind a kaleidoscope of thoughts, all of which refused to properly coalesce.

Jess extricated herself from Annie's hug and held Sam's shoulders, looking hard into his face as if searching for something. "Thank you."

He didn't like the frightened look in her eyes, wondered if she could see the same in his. "Jess, I…"

"I have to go," she said.

"I'll run you back on my bike," Phil offered.

"No," she said, backing away, "I need to get some air, clear my head. I'll see you all tomorrow."

Sam watched her go, his body almost vibrating with some kind of nervous energy that left a sour taste in his mouth. Someone patted his shoulder, told him well done but he didn't look away from Jess. She was almost at the end of the reception building when he ran after her. She didn't turn, to see who'd followed her and they were out of sight of the others by the time he caught up. There was a single light, midway along the road, the branches of a tree partially obscuring it to paint dancing shadows across the tarmac.

"Jess."

"I'm okay Sam," she said, without stopping, "honestly. Go back to the party, I'll be fine."

"But I need to talk to you."

Now she stopped. The light cast an aura around her head. Her eyebrows knitted together at the bridge of her nose. "What's up?"

However he played the conversation in his head, he sounded like a nutter and now he had her attention, he wasn't sure he wanted it. "When I grabbed you, did you feel anything?"

"What?" The knit between her eyebrows deepened a moment then softened. "Oh Sam, I'm so sorry, I'm seeing someone."

His confusion only lasted a moment. She thought he was a love-struck teenager. "No, I don't mean like that. I meant, did you feel anything when you fell and I caught you?" Because, he wanted to say but knew it was too much, that's what I saw in your eyes.

"I don't understand."

"When I grabbed your hand, something happened. I saw something I shouldn't have."

"Like what?"

"This isn't going to make sense."

"Sam," she said gently, "you're not making sense anyway. I mean, I know I'm all freaked out..." She fluttered her hands around her head, to illustrate her point. "But you've lost me."

"I saw you." Telling her straight, of course, was the best option. "You were near a railway line, perhaps at a train station."

"How could you have seen that?"

"You were wearing a flower print dress and there was a man, with a moustache and brown hair and he was pushing you onto the railway tracks and you were screaming and there was a train coming."

"What?" She looked scared. "What are you talking about?"

"This man, he was trying to hurt you."

"I don't understand what you're talking about. We're on the camp, you caught me on a bar, there's no train."

"I saw it when I held your hand. I saw you. You were terrified and falling into the path of a train."

"No." She shook her head, as if to keep his words away from her. "Just stop. I don't know what you're doing, but this is cruel."

"I'm not trying to be, I just need to tell you what happened. When you thanked me, you looked frightened. Did you see what I saw?"

"Of course I didn't, are you mad?"

"I don't know, I hope not. Nothing like this has ever happened to me before."

"I think it's a really shitty thing to do, Sam, so why don't you just fuck off and leave me alone? If you want to read futures, go and speak to Madame Rosa by the pier, she might want someone to look after her booth at lunchtimes."

She stalked away and he watched her go with a heavy heart, knowing he'd done the wrong thing completely but not sure how he could have done it differently. She turned the corner at the edge of the reception building and he was on the road alone. For a moment, the light flickered but he didn't want to turn towards it, in case someone was hanging under the blinking glow.

Footsteps came up behind him.

"What's up, Sam?" asked Polly.

"You wouldn't believe me if I told you."

"Try me." She looked earnest enough that he almost did believe she wouldn't laugh. If the situation were reversed and she was telling him this, he knew he'd laugh because it sounded so bloody insane. "Do you like her?"

"Of course, she's nice." It took him a moment to realise Polly had misread the situation about him fancying her too. "But not like that."

She looked away for a moment. "So what was it? Or don't you want to tell me? I can go back to the others, if you'd prefer."

"I do want to tell you, Polly but, more than anything, I just want to go home."

"That's fine, I'll walk with you." They started along the road and Polly was quiet until they turned the corner. "Have you thought about how to tell me yet? I'm curious what you could have said to make Jess shout at you."

"You'll laugh."

"How can you say that?"

"Because I would, if someone told me."

"I won't." She held up her little finger and flexed it. "Pinky swear."

"I'm being serious."

"So am I," she said, nodding gravely.

They shook pinkies. Even if she did laugh at him and their friendship went pear-shaped, he could hide out in the caravan for three days and avoid her if necessary. "When I grabbed Jess, I saw something." He clenched his fists, stretching his fingers that suddenly felt tight with anxiety.

"Like what?"

He told her and she listened attentively then puffed her cheeks to blow out a breath when he finished. "Holy shit."

"Well, you took it better than she did."

"But you can surely understand her reaction? That bloke you described sounds like her boyfriend and it must be harsh hearing that you saw him in a vision trying to throw her under a train."

"That's not what I said.

"It sounded like it to me." She still hadn't laughed at him. "Have you ever seen anything like this before?"

"No and it's fucking scary."

"Of course it is, you saw into the future."

He snapped her a look because she sounded serious, like she wanted to believe him. "I can't see the future, nobody can."

"Apart from psychics, mystics, mediums. The seaside's full of them, Sam, there's one near Roy's museum."

"Madame Rosa," he said, "Jess told me." They crossed the roundabout. "But this is the first time anything weird like this has happened to me." He stopped, realised it was a lie.

She stopped beside him. "What?"

"Last night," he said. "You didn't want me to walk you back to your caravan so I followed the road and the light started flickering. I heard this noise, like a rope swing then saw someone floating under the lamppost, but only when it was flickering. When it was properly on, they weren't there."

"You saw a ghost?" she asked, incredulous.

"I saw something I didn't understand."

Polly shivered. "You're just trying to scare me. You know I'm in the van on my own."

"I promise you. Until yesterday, nothing like this has ever happened to me before."

She looked at him aghast. "What if it's got something to do with bashing your head?"

"Don't be stupid."

"Roy thought you had concussion."

"Concussion doesn't make you see ghosts and have visions."

"Then what does?"

"I don't know," he said.

"Perhaps you should go to A&E, get yourself checked out."

"No, I'll be fine," he said and started walking again.

Mum was sitting on the step, smoking a cigarette. "Hey, Sammy, did you have a good evening?"

"It was okay."

She tilted her head, considering him. "That doesn't sound good."

He'd already made his mind up not to say anything because if he told her about the vision it might slip out about him bashing his head and then she'd have more to worry about than she already did. "I'm all right, it was just a bit weird."

"You and Polly are both okay, though?"

"Uh huh."

"Fair enough, well I'm sorry your night wasn't better."

"Thanks. How was yours?"

She compressed her lips. "I really did not have a good night."

"Are you okay?"

"I'll live."

"Where did you go?"

"Out with Frank again." She forced a smile that looked pained in the wan light. "Let's just say I won't be going on any more dates with that Prince Charming."

"Didn't go so well then?"

"No." She examined the glowing tip of her cigarette, took a long drag then flicked the ash by pulling a thumbnail over the filter. She hotched across the step and patted where she'd just moved from. "This might make you feel better. Sit down, I discovered that from here, you can see loads of stars."

Sam sat and looked up. The dark caravans around them hid the street lights and the trees behind the car park hid the lights of Barton Point. High up, stars glittered across the inky sky like diamonds.

"Cool, eh?"

"Yeah," he said.

She put her hand on his leg and squeezed, just above his knee. "We'll survive, Sammy."

"I know, Mum, I know."

Six

Sam woke to the sound of a gull disco dancing on the roof.

His head ached, a dull throb that pressed into his temples and he held them carefully as he sat up, draping his legs over the edge of the bed. Upright, the pain seemed to subside slightly and he stood up slowly and walked out of the bedroom.

Mum was eating cereal at the table and they exchanged waves as he went into the toilet. After peeing, he splashed water on his face and studied his reflection. There were no throbbing veins in his forehead, as he'd feared and something Polly said last night nagged at him – what if this was all caused by the bump?

"Morning, Sammy," Mum said as he went into the kitchen. "Sleep well?"

He'd woken up a couple of times when things seemed to knock against the caravan but had quickly drifted off again. "I think so, you?"

"Always weird sleeping in a new bed," she said.

"Would you like another coffee?"

She drained her mug and held it up. "Every time you ask."

He made her a drink and gave it to her, made himself a glass of orange squash, poured a bowl of Cornflakes, put the milk on, then sat across from her at the table.

She put her hand over his and rubbed briskly. "What shall we do on this, another glorious day on the east coast."

"The sun's not shining, Mum."

"At least it's not raining."

Someone knocked at the door.

"Oooh." Mum raised her eyebrows in exaggerated surprise, "I wonder who this could be?"

She went to open the door and exclaimed a hello. "So nice to see you, Polly, come in."

"Hello, Mrs Taylor, is Sam about?"

"Of course," Mum said and gestured towards the lounge.

Polly stood on the mat, clasping her hands in front of her stomach, fingers digging into a rolled up cagoule. She wore a black t-shirt for a band he'd never heard of and shorts.

"Hey," he said.

"Hey." They looked at one another awkwardly, the silence stretching uncomfortably. "What're you doing today?"

"Nothing planned," said Mum. "But so long as you two promise not to have any more painful silences like that, why don't you do something together?"

"Are you sure?" Sam asked.

"Certain. Now get dressed and leave me in peace to read my book."

The sky was full of grey cloud and felt too low, making Sam vaguely claustrophobic, but it was warm enough for shorts and a t-shirt – his had colourful geometric shapes on; he didn't own any band ones. He carried their cagoules in his rucksack.

"Let's ride into town, go and see Roy," Polly suggested as they walked between the caravans.

"I have enough for a few goes on the tuppenny falls if you want."

"You know how to show a girl a good time." When he glanced at her in surprise, she smiled. "You're so easy to wind up."

"You're just very good at it."

"Oh, really...?"

As they crossed the roundabout, he saw Jess behind the counter. She waved and they waved back.

"That's good," said Polly, "I wondered if she'd be a bit funny with us."

Relieved it wasn't just him that had whittled over it, he said, "Me too."

"Did you think any more about your vision?"

"Only most of the night," he said.

"Have you had any more?"

"I haven't touched anyone else."

Polly sat on the steps of Starz Bar and held out her hand. "Try me, then."

She wiggled her fingers, to encourage him and he rubbed the back of his neck, thoughts tumbling. What if he saw something terrible? On the other hand, for peace of mind, what if he didn't see anything at all?

"I don't know…"

"Come on, you baby," she said and grabbed his hand.

Nothing happened. He held out his other hand, wondering if he needed to complete a circuit and she took it but still nothing.

"No," he said with relief.

"Oh." Her disappointment weighed heavily on the word. "I did think, last night, that it might be because you were both scared, your emotions were all over the place. I love this kind of weird stuff and read that if you're agitated or anxious, really frightened or angry or whatever, it can open a channel into psychic ability."

"Is that true?" He couldn't hide his scepticism. His dad once said that if people could read futures they'd all be living on desert islands as millionaires. "I'm not sure I believe that."

"You don't believe in the supernatural, even after the vision and the dangling person in the light?"

He was scared of the idea of ghosts, as much as he loved scary stories and horror films, but did he really believe? And if he didn't, how could he explain what he'd experienced?

"I suppose so. Do you?"

"Yes, I do," she said, with conviction and let go of his hands. He felt the loss of contact keenly. She stood up and brushed off the seats of her shorts. "I believe completely."

"Well I'm glad nothing happened. I'd hate never being able to touch someone again, just in case I saw something terrible."

"You'd have to lock yourself away." She started walking. "Let's go and cadge a bike off Max."

They rode towards town on the Surrey bike, wind in their faces carrying the sharp tang of sea water. With no rain, there were more people on the beach, hardy souls braving the water to paddle and cars went by with little kids in the back waving at them.

Sam stole a glance at Polly. Her fringe had blown up from her forehead. She looked very happy.

The tide was in enough that the supports at the end of the old wooden pier were underwater. A man held a small boy who sat on the railings, letting a bucket down into the water.

"They're crabbing," Polly explained. "Do you like crab?"

"I've never had it."

"Oh it's delish, when we get into town you can buy me some and I'll share it with you."

"You know how to treat a man, don't you?" he teased and laughed when she faced him, her mouth a perfect 'o'.

A Talbot Avenger passed them and honked its horn, the driver gesturing towards the sea. Polly watched it go.

"Who was that?" Sam asked.

"My dad," she said and didn't sound happy, braking to a halt a few yards on from the pier entrance.

Sam turned in his seat and watched the car perform a sloppy three-point turn and come up to park behind them. Polly's dad got out and reminded Sam of Martin Fry from ABC, if Martin Fry wore a black leather jacket and jeans instead of his gold suit. Mr Dutton's hair was bleached blonde and brushed into a smart quiff that barely moved as he walked briskly to the bike.

"Morning love," he said, leaning on the frame. He glanced at Sam, who felt the chill in the man's glare. "Who's your friend?"

"This is Sam, he's staying on the camp with his mum."

"I see." Mr Dutton fixed him with a stare. "Been down here long?"

"Just a couple of days," Sam said. "We head home on Saturday morning."

"Had fun?"

"It's been okay," said Sam but the man's attention had already shifted.

"Where you going at this time of day?" Polly's dad asked her.

"Going to see Roy, then play in the arcades and Sam's never had crab before so we were going to get some for lunch."

"You shouldn't be treating boys, they should be paying for you. What did I tell you?"

Sam felt his cheeks burn with embarrassment and looked at his hands, his fingers fighting as he clasped them together.

"I'm not treating him," Polly said patiently, as if this was the kind of conversation she and her dad had all the time. "He's paying."

"Good, make sure you ain't paying out all your money, I don't work hard so he can enjoy it."

"I know that, Dad," she said, firmer than Sam would have expected. He felt horribly awkward, a reluctant witness to a dispute he imagined Polly wished she wasn't having.

"You need to be careful, running around with boys."

"Dad," she said, stretching the syllables.

"How old are you, son?"

"Sixteen."

"Yeah, I remember that age. Only thinking about one thing, am I right?"

"Dad," Polly said sharply, "you're embarrassing me. Sam's the same age as me."

"You have to be careful."

"I am careful, I'm always careful."

Mr Dutton tapped his lip with a finger, as if considering her answer.

"Where are you going?" she asked him, as if worried what he might say next otherwise.

Mr Dutton paused for a moment, as if Polly had somehow outsmarted him and he didn't know what to say. "Back to the van, to pick up some stuff."

"You haven't been back all week."

"It's been busy. We've had three meets at Yarmouth, a couple in Norwich and…"

"And I've been on my own for a week."

His tone softened. "I know that, but it is how it is, if I'm away, I can't get back."

They stared at one another for a few moments until he looked away.

"It's all money in the bank," he said. "You'll thank me for it later."

"Uh huh."

He pulled out his wallet. "Here, take this and enjoy that crab." He handed her a tenner and she took it reluctantly. "Go on, it'll do you good."

"Are you coming back tonight?"

"Can't," he said. "I've got to go, sweetheart, just be careful, okay?" He kissed his fingertips and pressed them to her forehead. With a vague nod towards Sam, he pushed away from the bike. "And ride carefully, these things can be deathtraps."

In the heavy silence, Sam looked towards the father and son crabbing on the pier as Polly drummed her fingers on the handlebars. The car started up and Mr Dutton drove by, swung into the junction and came back towards them with a curt wave and then he was gone.

Polly leaned forward and exhaled loudly.

"You okay?" Sam asked.

"Do I look okay?"

"Not really."

She shook her head. "He does it to me all the time. I swear to god, he forgets I fucking exist and then, when he remembers, he's annoyed because I'm getting on with my life."

She wasn't really talking to him so Sam didn't answer.

"Every year since…" She stopped, breathed. "All summer in that fucking caravan." She sat up straight in a brisk movement and fixed him with a glare. "I'm glad I spoke to you, I really am, because I like you and it's been exciting since I've known you, but I shouldn't have to be making new friends every week to stop being lonely, should I?"

He shook his head.

"No," she said for him and glanced over her shoulder. "Let's go."

They rode in silence for a while then she asked, "Is your dad still about?"

"Yes, but he walked out and started another family so we don't have much to do with each other."

"You're lucky. My mum had an accident when I was little, I don't remember anything about her at all, I just have memories I've made up from photographs."

"I'm sorry," he said because that's what he knew people said when they heard someone had died.

"Why? It wasn't your fault." He didn't know how to respond so kept quiet. She glanced at him. "Sorry, that was really shitty, I didn't mean it."

"I know."

"No you didn't." She wiped her face without looking at him. "This is exactly why I believe in ghosts, Sam, because if I do, I might get to see her again."

Seven

The Barton Point Museum Of Marvels looked dishevelled, the paint on the door and window frames peeling, the exhibits in the window covered with dust. A sheet of chipboard covered the window broken on Monday night. The front door was propped open by a hessian sack that had eyes and ears attached to it, like a little hobgoblin to welcome in the customers.

Polly steered the Surrey bike past the museum and turned into a side street.

"Where are we going?"

"Parking," she said and swung into a narrow alley that ended in a make-shift parking area, the ground pitted with holes, some of them patched up with gravel.

She slid out of the bike, said "come on then" and led him back around onto the beach road. As she went through the museum door, a bell tinkled somewhere and then something that sounded like a wild animal made a rumbling lowing sound.

"What the hell was that?" Sam asked, startled.

"Something marvellous, probably," she said with a smile.

The hallway was made narrower by shelves holding several piles of pamphlets and a huge stuffed owl, secured down with a chain around both ankles. The bird's feathers looked threadbare and the taxidermist had left it with a bewildered expression.

The foyer at the end of the hallway had two doors opening off it and a staircase leading up to the first floor. The air felt musty and dust motes danced in it.

"Are you about, Roy?" Polly called.

His voice drifted to them. "I am, I'll be there in a minute." Floorboards overhead creaked.

"I think you'll like it," she said, excitement in her voice, "I love this place. It's like all the books I read as a kid, the ghost stories and Arthur C. Clarke's Mysterious World, all come to life."

"What a marvellous description, Polly," said Roy as he came downstairs, carrying something. "Thank you."

He wore the same cardigan as Monday night, the two small pockets near the waist bulging with items. His cords were pressed, his shoes highly polished.

At the bottom of the stairs, he nodded at each of them in turn and held up the object he was carrying. It reminded Sam of the baton his school used in relay races.

"A press gang billy club," Roy said. "They used it to crew ships in the old days." He swished it through the air with surprising quickness. "That's one way to get you to sea, eh?" He smiled at Sam. "So good to see you again, my young friend. How's the noggin?"

"It's okay."

"I'm glad to hear it."

"Any chance of a cup of tea and a catch-up?" Polly asked.

"Splendid idea," said Roy and gestured for them to go into the room on the right.

A sailor, in full dress uniform, came through, glanced at Roy then looked curiously at Sam for an uncomfortably long moment, before heading quietly up the stairs.

"Come on," said Polly. "You look miles away."

Sam watched the sailor go up the stairs then followed Polly into a room filled with all manner of exhibits, on shelves and in glass cases. Roy opened a narrow door marked 'private' between two book cases and let them through.

This room was compact and windowless, with a small fridge in one corner, an array of cups on top of it. A small desk, chair and two-seat sofa filled the remainder of the space. Old posters for the Barton Point Variety theatre covered one wall. Newspaper clippings were pinned haphazardly to a green bulletin board.

"My inner sanctum," Roy said.

He sat at the desk and gestured Sam towards the sofa. Polly made them all tea – in proper cups, with saucers – then sat next to Sam. The cushions sank in the middle, tipping them towards one another slightly.

"So did you go and get yourself checked out?"

"No," said Polly, "he didn't."

Sam shot her a quick frown. "I didn't want to scare Mum."

"I understand," said Roy, "but I'd have been perfectly happy to take you myself."

"I know but…"

"He saw a ghost," said Polly eagerly.

Sam shot her another frown. What if Roy made the same connection she had, that the things he was seeing were connected to him bumping his head?

"Tell me more," Roy said, leaning forward.

Sam told his story and Roy listened intently.

"You've never seen anything like it before?"

Sam shook his head.

"You believe him, don't you?" Polly asked.

"I believe Sam believes it," said Roy. "Are you staying at the Good Times camp too?"

"Uh huh."

"Interesting. Would you give me a moment?" Roy excused himself and left the room.

"I didn't know you were going to tell him about the ghost."

"Why? It's right up his street."

"But what if he thinks I still need to get my head looked at?"

"He won't, don't worry." She didn't sound convinced.

Roy came back in carrying a slim hardback book. He sat and put on a pair of half-moon glasses then flipped through the pages gently until he reached the spot he was after.

"This is a book of local legends," he said, peering at them over the lenses. "Someone in the historical society wrote it a few years back and my Pam, who was a real nut for ghosts and hauntings, helped. One of the stories she ferreted out concerned Hanging Tree Lane, which used to be the road out of town and now forms part of the border for your caravan park. There used to be a crossroads, at the edge of the woods, with a big tree next to it." He tapped the page. "In the fourteenth century, suicide was a mortal sin and since the victims couldn't be buried in consecrated ground, they were buried at crossroads instead. Soon, gallows were erected at crossroads for a similar reason, since outlaws weren't wanted near holy spots."

"I read about this," said Polly. "They hung them so the spirit of the person would be trapped, not knowing which road to take to get away."

Roy nodded his agreement. "Pam went through all the documents in the historical society and found these reports, where people had either seen or felt something odd around this tree. When they re-did the road, they skirted around the wood completely and nature reclaimed it, as it will, but the park almost touches the edge of the crossroads. And some of the newer reports she found were from people who'd been on holiday, complaining about strange noises in the night or seeing people or shapes." He tapped the page again. "It's a good read. Pam knew how to get a story across."

"Great," Sam said, "now I'm never going to get to sleep."

Roy chuckled. "It's all about belief, like I said."

"I believe," said Polly, almost to herself. "How about you, Roy? Running this place, you must do."

"I believe people believe, but I don't any more. While life can sometimes inspire belief, it can also knock it."

"What do you mean?" asked Sam.

"Pam and I had a son called Roger. He served in the Navy but didn't come home from the Falklands. His passing strengthened her belief and dashed mine." Roy's eyes shone in the light.

Sam wondered if seeing that customer earlier, in his full naval dress, had brought back bad memories and that was the reason Roy had seemed to ignore him.

"Pam embraced the belief, wanted desperately to be receptive to it. I just knew that if there was any way Roger could let me know he was okay, he would do so. He never did and neither has Pam since she passed."

"I'm sorry," said Polly, "that's so sad."

He touched her arm. "No, it's life Polly. We all have to decide what we believe in."

"Yes," said Polly, "like the mermaid."

"You've got a mermaid?" Sam asked, incredulously.

"Indeed," Roy said proudly. "Do you want to see her?"

Polly stayed in the office, reading Pam's book, as Sam followed Roy upstairs. Three rooms opened off the first floor landing, two at the front of the building. The back room was a glorious mishmash of pictures, books and exhibits, with a large window overlooking the car park where they'd left the Surrey bike. A small table with a glass case on it stood in the middle of the room. Sunlight glittered off various bits of glass and ammonite on the shelves across from the window.

A shrunken head stood on a plinth on one shelf. Sam leaned in close, knowing it had to be fake, but it looked much more realistic than he'd expected.

"Dr Forrestal," said Roy. "He taught at the university in Norwich then went looking for some indigenous tribes in Central America and nobody heard from him for several years, before his wife received this in the post."

Sam smiled at the tale. "Do you have a story for all of your exhibits?"

"Of course, my boy."

"So how did the indigenous tribespeople find a post office?"

Roy held up his finger. "You're the first person to ask me that question in a long, long time and you should always ask the question."

"So you're like a scientist and need proof?"

Roy smiled and held out his arms. "Looking at my museum, you're the first person who's ever compared me to a scientist." He moved to a glass case on the table. "Though here's a scientific marvel, the world famous Barton Point mermaid."

Sam looked into the dusty case. A small skeleton, with a skull, arms and what looked like a ribcage, lay on black velvet. But rather than legs, a fish tail completed the body. "Wow," said Sam.

"At the turn of the last century," Roy said, "two little girls were rockpooling and came across this curious little creature. They told their father and he, a doctor of repute, took the creature back to his surgery but it sadly died soon after. He wrote to colleagues in a large university hospital in London about it and then received a visit from a scientist and a man from the ministry. Neither could positively identify the skeleton, though they shared their belief but this was kept strictly off the record. The doctor died in action during the First World War and his daughters, years later, passed the skeleton on to the museum before they passed." He touched the glass gently. "For years, it was the centrepiece of my displays and during the early 70s we gained a bit of notoriety for it."

"How can it be a mermaid?"

"How can it not be, when you can see it with your very own eyes?" Roy pointed to a high contrast black and white photograph on the wall, showing a man in a hat and collar standing with two young girls on a beach. "The good doctor," he said, "with his daughters."

"That's them?"

Roy looked at him gravely, clearly trying not to smile. "Of course not," he said, with good humour. "When we opened the museum, I needed something to draw attention and as we were renovating the rooms, we found the skeleton of a cat. I remembered Barnum's Fiji mermaid and went to the fishmongers and bought the biggest cod I could find and there we have it."

"I knew it wasn't real."

"But you believed, for a moment. Just like people believed it when we first opened. Finding that picture, of someone with his daughters, was the icing on the cake. My point, Sam, is that just because you don't believe something, doesn't mean it isn't there."

"A fake mermaid is a bit different from a ghost in a caravan park."

Eight

Polly showed him around until lunchtime and Sam didn't see any other customers, even the sailor. She offered to treat Roy to lunch but he'd already made his sandwiches – "waste not, want not" – and suggested a crab stall run by a friend of his.

There was a wispy element of rain in the air when they left the museum, as if the weather had to justify the dark clouds somehow. Pulling on their cagoules, they walked up to the funfair and queued at the crab stall. It took ten minutes to get served – Polly assured Sam a queue at a fish place at the seaside was a good sign – and the owner, when they told him Roy had sent them, undercharged Polly by at least half. They ate sitting in nearby bus shelter.

Roy was right, the crab was perfect and Sam was an instant convert.

By the time they'd polished off a portion of chips between them, the clouds were starting to break up, small patches of vivid blue visible between the grey and Polly suggested going back to The Golden Nugget.

They walked back towards the museum, smiling at the children who explored the toys hanging off awnings and delved into the buckets of balls and cricket sets and tennis rackets that crowded the doorways of the tourist shops.

As they crossed the side street Polly had steered the Surrey bike into, Sam heard brakes screech. A car pulled up sharply, its nearside wheel up on the kerb. He couldn't see the passenger, light reflecting off the window but the driver was already halfway out his door. The man glared at Sam, teeth bared under his moustache.

"Oi, you little shit."

Instantly recognising him, Sam's stomach lurched and his heart hammered against his chest. The man he'd seen in the train station with

Jess walked around the front of the car, his white-flecked dark suit at odds with the thunderous look on his face.

Lips tight against his teeth, the man jabbed a finger at Sam. "Who the hell do you think you are, scaring my girl like that? I ought to knock you out right now."

Fear gathered in Sam's throat and he wanted to throw up. Or faint.

"What girl?" shouted Polly. "You've got the wrong person."

The passenger door opened and Jess tried to get out, the seatbelt wrapped around her arm. "Bill," she shouted, "leave it."

Showing no sign he'd heard, Bill grabbed Sam's arm

Sam tried to shake him off but the grip was too strong. "Let go of me," he called. His eyes felt hot and he hoped he wasn't going to start crying. "What're you doing?"

Bill shoved him back and Polly skipped neatly out of the way as he clattered into a door. She grabbed Bill's arm.

"Leave him alone," she shouted.

Jess came up behind him, pulling on his shoulders. "Bill, get off him!"

"I didn't do anything," Sam protested. He couldn't prise Bill's fingers away.

Bill shook Jess off. "Jess told me what happened last night, that she was going to get hit by a train and I wouldn't save her. Are you fucking nuts?"

If he was this angry over the vision, Sam had the horrible feeling it might have been true. But how did he get out of this? Pushed against the door, his options were limited to kicking Bill in the nuts and hoping that gave him a chance to run.

"You're nuts," said Polly, "grabbing someone on the street like this."

Sam took the fire of her words, channelling his fear into anger. He had to stand up to this man, not be cowed, however terrified he might really be. "I told her what I saw," he said and suddenly saw something in Bill's eyes. Not vulnerability but maybe fear? He'd caught the man off guard and he was clearly scared. Sam took his chance and dug his nails into the back of Bill's hand, who released him with a yelp.

"Get away from me, you nutter," Sam said, adrenaline charging through him. He wasn't going to be pushed around, not like he was by Tracksuit and Thin man. Bill wasn't going to be given the chance to hurt him.

"Bill, come on." Jess pulled on his arm. "There'll be trouble."

He glanced at her then took a step back, glaring at Sam. "You should be locked up, you fucking psycho, telling people stuff like this." He jabbed a finger into Sam's shoulder.

Sam pushed him back. "If you touch me again, I'll go to the police and tell them that you are going to hurt her."

"And they'll laugh you out of the station."

He was right, of course but Sam needed something. "Unless something does happen, then they'd be really interested, wouldn't they?"

"Nothing's going to happen to her, you twat."

Bill went to jab him again but Sam caught his hand. The vision was instantaneous and rocked him back against the door.

Jess wore her flower print dress and looked so pretty it made his heart beat faster. But he felt angry too, the emotion burning his throat and chest. Jess was backing towards the edge of the platform and he saw his hands reaching for her. She looked terrified but he kept going anyway. He grabbed her wrist. The train horn sounded, so loud it was almost deafening. Still he pushed Jess back and knew, in a moment or two, that she would fall into space. Fall into the path of the train that wasn't stopping at this station.

Sam pushed Bill away, letting go of his hand like it was molten metal. The vision snapped off, leaving a throbbing pain in Sam's temple and a sour taste in the back of his throat. He groaned, retched, swallowed back bile.

"It was you," he said, his head feeling too heavy to lift up.

"What the fuck's he talking about?" muttered Bill.

"What did you do to him?" demanded Jess.

"Get away from me," Sam shouted, "and keep away from Jess too. I saw what you're going to do."

"You fucking freak, I haven't done anything."

"You did enough," said Polly. "I'll go to the police."

Jess pulled Bill back. "Leave it," she shouted, her voice cracking. She pulled him hard and he staggered back a couple of steps. "I'm sorry," she said, reaching out to touch Sam's arm but stopping just before she made contact. "I didn't realise what he'd do…"

"Come on," said Bill and pulled Jess back.

"Yeah, fuck off you chicken," said Polly, pressing a hand against Sam's chest, as if to stop him making a rash move.

Sam watched Bill as he backed towards the car. Jess watched him, eyes wide and scared. Bill opened her door, helped her in then rushed around to the driver's side. He revved the engine and the car lurched into the road.

Weak and nauseous, his adrenaline fading, Sam collapsed against the door, taking deep breaths. Polly put her hand on his back, her presence anchoring him to a reality he needed to embrace, a friend on a street in a seaside town and not some train station, where a madman was going to hurt Jess.

"Are you okay?" she asked.

"No." People who'd stopped to stare at the display began to move away, talking amongst themselves. Across the street, the blonde woman from the caravan park, still wearing her white t-shirt and red jeans, stared at him.

"Are you okay to walk?" Polly asked.

"I think so." He didn't feel right but taking a step didn't make him feel sick, so that was a good sign. He took another step.

The blonde woman still stared.

"What?" Sam asked, holding out his arms towards her.

The woman's eyes widened with surprise.

"Take a fucking picture," he shouted, "it'll last longer."

"Who're you talking to?" Polly asked as they walked back towards the bike.

Nine

Sam's mind swirled with anger and embarrassment and when Polly caught his arm he shook it off.

"Hey," she said indignantly, "you don't have to be a shit with me."

She was right but he didn't want her to touch him, didn't want to see anything else awful. It terrified him enough what he'd seen to people he didn't really know or care about, but what if he saw something awful about her? "No, you're right, I'm sorry."

She reached for him again but he moved his arm out the way. "What's going on, Sam?"

"It happened again, when I touched his hand."

"Oh," she said.

"Polly, it was horrible, the other view of what I saw last night. He shoved her and she fell."

"Sam, it's…"

"Something I couldn't have seen? I know."

"It was all his fault?"

"I saw him push her."

Her eyes darted as she took in all his face before looking away, as if worried about what she might see. "None of this makes any sense, Sam."

"Don't you think I know that? It's impossible and I wish it wasn't happening but it is. You do believe me, don't you?"

Now she did look at him. "Yes, absolutely. I mean, why would you make it up?"

"Because I'm going mad? Because I got bumped on the head?"

"People bump their heads all the time and nothing like this happens to them. Why would you become psychic because you fell over?"

"I'm not psychic."

"What do you call it then?"

"I couldn't see anything weird when I held your hand yesterday, could I? And I absolutely don't want to try again, just in case."

"It is based on emotions then. You and Jess were frightened last night and, just now, Bill was angry and you were being bullied. If we get scared or angry, our brains don't always do logical things."

"So I cracked something when I fell?"

She looked frustrated, pushed into a dead end by her own words. "I don't know."

"There's no pain there," he said, pressing his fingers against the back of his skull. His temples still ached with a dull throb he'd mostly forgotten about, but there wasn't any kind of stabbing pain that would indicate trouble.

"Let me see."

"No," he said, too sharply and she shrank away, making him feel worse. "I'm sorry, but I don't want to touch you and see something."

"But it didn't work on me before, did it? And we're not all wound up."

Reluctantly, he stooped down so she could reach. He felt her fingers on his hair and gently touching his scalp. It didn't take her long to reach a conclusion. "Nothing there, you're right."

"I'm going mad, aren't I?"

They rode back to the camp in awkward silence, the rain starting again as they passed the old pier, pattering on the canvas roof of the bike. It was mid-afternoon and the few families who'd braved the weather on the beach were finally giving up the ghost, traipsing dispiritedly up the sand, pulling children who clearly didn't want to go.

"Do you think we should tell the police?" Polly asked, glancing at him.

"How do we make them believe me? I'm a teenager, they'll say I'm larking about. I'll probably get into trouble for wasting their time."

"But you're not."

"We know that, but they won't. And this is what it'll always be like, if this keeps happening. I see stuff that's going to happen to people but when I try to warn them, they won't believe me. I'll end up in a freak show, or working for this Madame Rosa on the pier like Jess said last night."

"I believe you what you're saying to me," she said.

He felt heat behind his eyes and nose as his emotions built. The lane to the camp was a hundred yards or so ahead but tears clouded it. "What am I going to do, Polly?" A tear ran down his cheek and he wiped it angrily away.

"Are you crying?" she asked softly.

"No."

She applied the brake and pulled them into a layby, the tyres crunching over gravel. Out of sight, kids shrieked as they played a game.

"Sam, don't get upset, we can sort this."

"But we can't, because I can't control it. What if I have to live the rest of my life not touching people? What if I can never hug Mum again, just in case I see something horrible in her future."

Polly quickly took his hands in hers. He tried to push her away but she held on tighter, staring at him. "Do you see anything? Sam, focus on me, on my face. Do you see anything?"

He tried to shut her out, the keen look in her eyes, the determined set of her jaw, the feel of her warm skin against his. He heard the rain on the canvas, felt a cool breeze on his neck, saw the tops of the trees moving. Everything he was experiencing, at that moment, was in the real world he could see or feel or touch. "No."

She held his hands tighter. "What am I thinking about?"

"I don't know."

"Look me in the eyes," she insisted, "and tell me what I'm thinking."

He looked into her eyes but his only reaction was to think how lovely they looked, how bright and full of vitality. He thought how he'd like to sit here and look into her eyes for a long time. "I can't tell."

"Then I was right, Sam, you're reacting to emotion. When you were scared, your mind picked up on something, the same when you were frightened and angry. It could be something like a really vivid daydream, a brain fart or something as your mind tries to keep you safe."

"A brain fart almost got me beaten up today?"

She giggled briefly. "Okay, so that didn't come out the way I meant it."

"But I knew him, from the vision with Jess."

"Maybe you saw him around and didn't realise." She lightly shrugged her shoulders and growled softly. "I'm trying to help you here, you idiot," she said and pulled a face until he smiled.

Max wasn't in his hut as they rode around the corner and into the car park. In the daylight, the height bar looked ridiculously high and much narrower than it had seemed last night.

"Don't think about it," advised Polly as she skidded the bike into place, braking at the very last moment and slid off the seat.

Sam got out and zipped up his cagoule, looking at the back of reception. He could see the office through the window but nobody in there. Was she back on shift or had she got the day off with Bill? Was she thinking about last night, or about what Bill had just done? Whatever she'd told him, it clearly lit a fire so even if Polly was right and Sam had experienced some kind of waking dream, he'd somehow touched a nerve.

They walked around the corner of the arcade and cut across the playpark, as if both of them wanted to avoid Jess.

"Are you going back to say hello to your mum?"

"Probably." He ought to, since they'd come on holiday for a break from life at home, not from each other.

"Did you want to meet up later?"

"Shall I call for you?"

She touched his arm. "I'll come and get you. The last thing I need is some snitch telling Dad I'm having eligible lads knocking on my door." She smiled enigmatically and walked away, waving her fingers over her shoulder.

Ten

Gone into town for a breath of fresh air. Taken my book, might stay all afternoon. If we're back at the same time, I'll make us some dinner. Love you, Sammy.

Mum

He spent the afternoon in the lounge reading his horror anthology, trying to shake the confrontation with Bill from his mind. It mostly didn't work.

Mum pulled up in the early evening though the cloud was so thick and dark by then it looked like night had already fallen. At least the rain had stopped.

Polly came around the side of another caravan and they stood chatting for a while, far enough from the window he could only hear a low murmur, then came into the van bringing the scent of fresh air, the sea and perfume.

Mum dropped her bag and keys on the kitchen counter and slipped off her anorak. "I'm busting for a pee."

Polly smiled crookedly at her as Mum went into the toilet. "Hey you."

"Hey."

"How're you feeling?"

"All right, I suppose."

"Good." She sat across from him on the sofa, putting her hands under her thighs. "I'm okay, too." Smiling, she dipped her head towards him. "You can ask me, you know."

"Ask you what?"

"How I'm feeling. It's a thing boys can say to girls and who knows, when you go into Sixth Form, it might make you a babe magnet."

"How do you know I'm not already?"

"Because I had to remind you to ask if I'm feeling okay."

Mark West

Mum came out of the toilet. "I don't fancy cooking so how about we push the boat out and I'll treat you to a night at the Starz Bar."

Sam was surprised. Since the divorce, Mum often told him their money situation was "tighter than a gnat's chuff" and that meant only the occasional treat to a Wimpy.

"I'd like that," said Polly, "so long as you let me treat you."

"I couldn't do that."

"You could if I told you I haven't spent all the guilt money Dad gave me today."

"Then I'd be pleased to let you treat me."

In the small foyer of The Starz Bar, Annie sat behind a table selling tickets for a meat raffle to be held at the end of the night and checked people's keys to make sure they weren't punters coming for free entertainment from another camp. She smiled at Polly and Sam. Mum bought a raffle ticket and said she was looking forward to a nice bit of squirrel. Annie frowned at her.

The venue hadn't been decorated in a long time. The bar took up most of the left side of the room with a handful of people sitting on stools nursing pints. Two Big D peanut boards hung over the cash till, the modesty of the model on both still protected by unsold packets.

A dance floor, surrounded on three sides by tables and chairs, filled the middle of the room and little kids were holding skidding contests on the polished floor. A low stage took up the right side of the room and a three-piece band played easy listening to a disinterested audience, the guitarist and keyboard player looking bored, the drummer gurning for all he was worth. The lighting and sound rig, as Polly had told him before, was no better than school disco quality. A mirror ball hung over the dance floor and tatty strands of tinsels, that seemed to have survived a post-Christmas clean-up, clung to the ceiling tiles.

"Get us a seat, love," Mum said to Polly, "and I'll get the first round in. I'm having a wine, what did you want?"

"Wine."

"Do you drink often?"

"Only when there's a responsible adult about."

"I'm fairly responsible," Mum said.

Polly chose a table and sat facing the bar. Sam sat across from her. "Are you glad you finally got into this entertainment mecca, then?"

He laughed. "Your description was spot on."

"You should have believed me."

Mum came back carrying a round tray. She set it down, handed Polly her wine and a bottle of Strongbow to Sam. "Apparently, it's glamorous granny night tomorrow." She looked around. "Remind me not to come in, I think I'm the oldest here."

"No you're not," said Polly, looking around too.

"You're lovely," Mum said, "but you're also clearly blind."

By the time most tables were occupied, the average age of the room had more than doubled and Mum stopped worrying. She was in good form too, helped by a couple of glasses of wine, as the three of them chatted and laughed easily.

When Mum decided it was time to eat, Sam got a menu from the bar. It had very limited choice and after they all decided on fish and chips, Mum went to order them.

"Shit," said Polly. "Don't turn around, but Jess has just come in."

Sam's stomach lurched. "Oh no, is he with her?"

"No, she's on her own and looking for someone."

Sam watched Polly's eyes move as she watched Jess. "She's talking to your mum."

"You're kidding?"

"No, when I'm kidding, I look like this." She pulled a face that elicited a quick laugh from him and made her smile. "She's coming over."

"Oh no." His stomach sank further. Surely Jess wouldn't cause a scene in here? If she did, Mum would want to know what had been going on and then everything would come out. Nothing good could come out of this situation, he decided. "Is she really?"

Polly nodded then looked up. "Ten seconds," she said, barely moving her lips. Her eyes widened with pretend surprise.

Sam was aware of movement and then Jess stood at the edge of the table. "Hi, you two," she said awkwardly. "Sam, could I have a word?"

He looked at her, wanting to say she could tell him whatever it was in front of Polly but said "yes" instead. She had a dark mark below her eye. Had Bill given her a black eye after the confrontation at the arcade?

She gave Sam a relieved smile, which didn't help the sensation of butterflies growing in his belly.

As he stood up, Polly raised her eyebrows. "Tell Mum I'll be back in a minute," he said.

"Yeah, right."

Sam followed Jess, trying to look everywhere at once, ready for Bill to come rushing at him. Mum, thankfully, had her back to him as she ordered food. In the foyer, Jess said something to Annie as she went outside.

The night air had cooled. Jess went down the steps and Sam followed cautiously, still looking. They seemed to be on their own. She went into the play park and sat on one of the swings.

"Sit next to me."

"Where's Bill?"

"I'm on my own, I promise."

Keeping a watchful eye, he sat on a swing, leaving one empty between them, the chain rattling as he settled himself.

"Before I start, I need you to know I'm really sorry about what happened earlier, Sam, and Bill is too. He wanted to come and apologise, but I told him that wouldn't be a good idea."

It felt like she was telling the truth and he wanted to believe her, which made him think of Roy and the mermaid. "Did he apologise for that too?" he said and gestured towards her face.

"No," she said with a gentle smile as she touched her eye softly, "he didn't."

Again, he believed her, but still the butterflies fluttered. "So what happened?"

"Would you believe me if I said I walked into a door?"

"I don't know."

"Well that's what I did."

He stared at his feet, willing himself to think of something intelligent and adult to say but nothing came.

"Sam, I have no reason to lie to you, do I? Bill didn't hit me, as much as he must have seemed scary to you."

"He bloody did," he said, then realised he sounded like a kid. "I mean, I was worried, but he properly scared Polly."

"I'll get him to apologise to her too." Jess pressed her feet into the groove dug by thousands of kids who'd used the swing in the past and pushed herself backwards. "I shouldn't have told him what happened but you scared me and by the time I'd got back to our flat, he could see it in my face. I didn't expect him to do anything about it today but as we drove by, for some reason I pointed you out and all hell broke loose." She swung a couple of times then stopped when she was raised up. "He didn't mean it."

"It looked like he did to me," he said, indignant she was trying to play it down.

"Honestly, he didn't but you really scared me last night. I don't believe in mystics and all that rubbish but you really saw something, didn't you?"

"I'm not sure. Polly reckons I was so scared I had a waking dream."

"Maybe," Jess said, "but you couldn't have known how close you were."

"In what bit?"

"Nobody knows this," she said, her voice dropping to a whisper, "but we're going away. I haven't even told Mum or Dad yet. The thing is, there are some bad memories here for Bill and we're going to make a fresh start."

"Okay." He didn't know why she was telling him this.

"Bill's already got the train tickets."

The penny dropped. "Oh."

"And now you can see why I got so freaked out?"

He tried to keep his expression neutral. If she knew he'd had a similar vision of Bill, would she freak out even more? "I do."

"And you've never had this happen before?"

He shook his head.

"Weird and a bit scary." Jess swung herself again.

Sam let himself swing back and forth. Was she waiting for him to say something else? They sat in silence for a moment or two.

"What are Bill's bad memories about this place?" he asked

She glanced at him, wrinkled her nose. "Bits and pieces." She took a deep breath, steeling herself and let it out slowly. "He's a bit older than me, almost thirty and…"

"How old are you?"

"Twenty-three. And his wife was older still, somewhere in her late thirties. She was really jealous, treated him badly and it seems like she used to slap him around. Anyway, she was having some problems, lost her job and took her own life."

"How?"

Jess bit her lip and shook her head again. "She jumped off a bridge as a train was coming."

He remembered the look in Jess' eyes before the train barrelled into his line of vision, wiping her completely from view in a mist of red. "Shit."

"Uh huh. There was talk about her being depressed and then rumours started that Bill might have been knocking her about which, clearly, couldn't be further from the truth because she was doing that to him. But Barton Point is a small community, that kind of thing sticks, so he wanted to get away. And I've lived here all my life, I want to see something of the world that doesn't involve me working in a reception and helping out in the arcade for six months a year." She looked at him, smiled sadly. "I'm telling you all this and I shouldn't be, I'm sorry Sam.

I just wanted you to understand, Bill was angry but not at you specifically, it was just everything building up."

Surely he had to tell her what he'd seen from Bill's vision? "And you really trust him?"

She looked like he'd suggested the sky was green. "Of course, I'm not a fool. If I didn't, I wouldn't be with him." She shook her head, as if trying to dislodge negative thoughts. "You said it yourself, Sam, it was a waking dream. Bill's nice to me, he wouldn't do anything…"

"I'm not saying he would, but I had no idea about any of this when I saw it, did I?"

"So now you're saying it was a vision?"

"No, but I think you should be careful."

"Wouldn't it look a bit suspicious if his first wife dies under a train and then his girlfriend does?"

Sam shrugged, caught in an impossible situation. To tell her his vision of Bill would mean he believed what he'd seen, which was clearly ridiculous, but if he didn't and something happened to her, what then?

"I appreciate your concern, I really do." She touched his knee and the contact sent a pleasant shiver up his leg. "It means a lot and would mean even more if you don't say anything to anyone until we're gone."

"I won't."

She stood up, holding the swing steady by its chain. "Thank you for this, Sam and for last night too. You were very brave to help me."

She gave him a quick peck on the cheek then walked away into the darkness of the lane.

Sam got back to the table just as the food turned up.

"There you are," said Mum.

"I told your mum you were helping Jess do something on the computer," Polly said quickly.

"Yes," he said, "that's right." He was taking computer studies at school and Mum was aware of them through his interest but had never used one herself. "All sorted now."

"Good."

The meal was nice but lukewarm at best, as if someone had biked it in from one of the chip shops in town. Sam wondered if, even now, Max was panting as he parked the Surrey bike. By the time they'd finished, the bar had filled steadily and there were plenty of people showing their abilities – or lack thereof – on the dance floor.

At a little after ten, Mum looked at her watch. "I'm going to head back, have an early night and read for a bit. Are you two okay to stay on for a while on your own?"

"Let me walk you home."

"Sam, I'll be fine. Just make sure Polly gets home safely and I'll see you soon."

Mum gave Polly a quick hug, ruffled Sam's hair – and laughed when he complained and re-styled it with his fingers – and left.

"I really do like your mum," Polly said and leaned forward. "Now what happened with Jess?"

He told her everything and she listened intently.

"Walked into a door," she said, shaking her head when he finished. "And you believed her?"

"No, but it seemed like she was telling the truth."

"Of course it did. Shit, this is bad."

"But what can we do?" He shrugged. "I mean, do we just let it go?"

She didn't say anything but looked dubious. The band finished their song with a flourish and the keyboard player leaned forward, too close to the microphone.

"And now for something up to date," he said.

"This should be fun," Polly said.

They began playing *I Want To Break Free*.

"Not that up to date," Sam said.

"They tried *Like A Virgin* last week," Polly said with a smile. "Cleared the floor in seconds."

After finishing a rousing version of *The Birdie Song*, the keyboard player launched into the sax solo from *Careless Whisper*. The dancefloor cleared of kids.

"Did you want to dance?" Sam asked.

"No," she scoffed and then looked at him, eyes wide. "I mean, unless you want to?"

He felt about an inch tall. "No, it's okay, I just wondered…"

"We'll just go," she said into the uncomfortable silence.

Annie tried to sell them raffle tickets as she said good night and it felt even cooler outside than before, Polly rubbing her arms as she went down the steps.

"Did you want me to walk you back?"

"You're determined to find my caravan, aren't you?" she teased.

"No," he said, trying to play it cool, "just trying to be a gentleman."

"Well stop, it doesn't suit you."

She stood on tiptoes, kissed his cheek quickly and then jogged across the roundabout, waving over her shoulder. "See you tomorrow?"

"Sure," he said, watching her go. Once she was out of sight, he followed the road around the edge of the camp, his mind replaying that last conversation with Polly. Was she teasing him about stopping being a gentleman, or suggesting he was being slow? Should he have tried harder to get her to do a last dance? Why didn't he say yes, when she asked if he wanted to?

An owl hooted in the woods, surprising him out of his thoughts.

The street light at the end of the road was out. There were no lights on in any of the vans and he couldn't hear any people making their way home. He felt, for one awful moment, as if he was all alone and that thought stroked the back of his neck like an icy finger.

A breeze blew, rustling leaves, the sound much louder than it should have been. He kept walking, gravel and dirt crunching under his trainers.

The owl hooted again and something moved in the hedge. He stepped away, imagining some kind of monster even though he knew it was probably only a hedgehog.

There was a thud from in amongst the caravans and a shadow cast across the road.

He stopped, watching. For the shadow to be there, someone surely had to be hiding behind the end of the caravan he was about to walk by. Why would they be hiding there? Could it be Bill?

Another step and the shadow stretched further, almost to the hedge now.

It had to be Bill. Jess was wrong, he did have murder in mind and needed Sam out of the way.

The shadow moved again so Sam ducked into the gap between caravans nearest him, rushing back to his own. He had the key out before he got there and quickly opened the door.

Mum had left the kitchen light on and he could hear her soft snores from her bedroom as he hurried inside.

He locked the caravan door behind him.

Eleven

High hedges on either side of the narrow lane blocked his view of everything other than a brilliantly blue, cloudless sky.

A woman shouted, clearly terrified. He ran, thinking he recognised her voice.

The road twisted, this way and that, until it seemed to become a maze. When the woman shouted again, she was nearer. A whistle sounded.

He ran faster, trainers slapping the road, his breathing loud and harsh.

Out of the last twist, the road arched up and over a railway line, its abutments like ornate gateposts. Polly stood halfway across the bridge, screaming, holding onto Mum's legs. Mum stood on top of the brick parapet, wobbling precariously.

The whistle split the air again, the train close now.

"Grab her legs," shouted Polly, "quickly."

He had no energy left, his legs like lead. The engine noise filled his senses, rattled his teeth.

Mum jumped, disappearing from view so quickly it was like she'd been erased. Polly, clinging on, was pulled sharply over the parapet.

The train whistle blew again, a shrill blast of victory.

Sam opened his eyes, shocked awake by the dream.

He was in bed, his heart racing, a cold sweat in his hairline. He held his breath and, from next door, could hear Mum's gentle snores. She was there, she was safe.

The curtains let in the greyest of light and he knew he wasn't alone in the room. There was a strange scent in the air, almost an earthy smell, the tang of Autumn leaves.

Startled, he pushed back against the wall. He couldn't see anyone, or hear them breathing, it was a sensation of being watched. Gently, he prodded the thin mattress of the upper bunk and it moved easily. Unless someone was crouching at the far end, no one was above him.

Which didn't leave anywhere for someone to be hiding.

That dream must have scared the absolute shit out of him. Relieved, he closed his eyes and flopped back on the bed. It must be an accumulation of everything, the visions, Bill's reaction and what Jess had said.

But he couldn't shake the sensation someone was in the room with him.

He opened his eyes.

The blonde woman crouched beside the bed, her head level with his. Grey shadows played across her cheekbones, cloaking the left side of her face in pale darkness.

Sam shrieked and pushed himself back but the wall and frame of the bunk beds stopped his escape.

The woman's eyes opened wide. "You can really see me," she said slowly.

Sam's heart raced, goosebumps rippling his arms. Fear squeezed his lungs, making it almost impossible to take a breath. "What are you doing in my room?"

She put an index finger to her lips.

Through the wall, Mum moaned and said something he couldn't understand.

Sam closed his eyes, pressing his fingernails into his palms, trying desperately to bring himself out of this waking nightmare.

"That won't help, I'll be here when you open your eyes."

He whimpered, pressed until his palms ached but he wasn't going to wake up because he was awake already.

"I have forever, so open your eyes."

"Please, go away." He didn't want to believe she was there but begging couldn't hurt. "Please."

"I need your help. You're the first person who's ever seen me."

"I don't want to see you."

"Charming, but I'll forgive you. I won't hurt you."

He slowly opened his eyes. The woman had moved back slightly, more of her face in shadow. His heart rate slowed a little but he still couldn't breathe properly.

"You shouted at me, earlier, outside the arcade when you met my husband Bill."

"Your husband…" Now it felt like someone was sitting on his chest. "This can't be happening."

"Well it is, I'm dead and yet somehow you can see me." She edged into the strip of pale light and he saw her dark jeans and white t-shirt. It was the woman from reception, from the car park on the night of the roof run and the one he'd shouted at. He was clearly going insane.

"My name's Gwen Morgan. I died but I'm doomed to stay here, watching my wretched husband live his life, the rage building inside me." She shook her head. "Sometimes, the dead need closure, they need to resolve an issue. It happens a lot, you'd be surprised at how many of us are about." She ran a hand through her hair. "Can you imagine an existence where you need to right a wrong and avenge your death and you can't get anyone to see you, or even hear you?"

He couldn't breathe in properly, air squeaking in his throat and it made him feel faint. He wondered if he was going to have a heart attack.

"I couldn't be sure you saw me from the roof, couldn't bear to believe it but then, when you shouted at me, I knew." She came closer, her earthy scent filling his nose as he tried to press himself further into the wall. "Please," she said, holding out a hand, "be still. What's your name?"

"Sam."

"I'm not going to hurt you, Sam." She moved forward, her hand getting horribly close to his face. "But you've hurt yourself. Not today, but very recently – your head." She moved her hand over his head without touching him. "Yes, I see an aura. There's damage here, at the back."

"What do you mean damage?"

"I don't know, I'm not a doctor."

Did she mean he was seeing a ghost because he'd hurt his head? Was that the cause of the visions too? Was he dying and seeing this woman because he was about to become a ghost himself? "Am I dying?"

"I told you, I'm not a doctor. The thing is, you're alive and you can help me to help Jess."

"How?"

"She's in danger." Gwen sat cross-legged on the floor. "Bill is a bully and an abuser, charming as anything on the outside but scary as fuck inside. He made me do things that…" She curled her lip and shook her head. "He's a nasty piece of work who made me lie about where my bruises came from, made me little more than a slave. One day I tried to get away but he caught up with me and put me in his car and drove out to the little lane with the railway bridge. I begged and pleaded and cried and promised to be a good girl but he still pushed me over." She looked at her shoes. "I came back the next day, stuck in this godforsaken town, unable to interact with anyone, just watching him live his life and lie to everyone. They said I'd taken my own life, that I'd been depressed for a long time. Of course I was fucking depressed, I'd been abused for years, wouldn't you be?"

She widened her eyes at Sam, as if expecting an answer. He nodded in agreement, not sure if that was right or wrong.

"Everyone believed him, showed him sympathy. He's come out the other side and started again and I worry for Jess, I really do. You saw what he's like."

"She has a black eye."

Gwen looked surprised. "He's getting careless then. My cuts and bruises were always out of sight, or easily hidden by a high collar or long sleeves. He never marked my face, though I could tell sometimes he just wanted to punch me in the mouth." She looked away, as if trying to dislodge painful memories. "Your friend is in danger. Bill's unpredictable, she must realise that but maybe she can't do anything about it. Perhaps she's like me, caught up in something she can't control."

"That's terrifying."

"What made him react so badly to you, was it jealousy?"

"This is going to sound stupid," he said then realised he was talking to a ghost. Nothing would sound stupid ever again. "That night in the car park behind the Starz Bar, I thought Jess was going to fall and she was scared too and when I grabbed her hand, I had some kind of vision."

"And what was it?"

"Her falling under a train."

Gwen blanched. "Go on," she said.

"I saw Bill too but didn't know it was him then. She told him and that's why he grabbed me today."

"You need to help her, Sam."

"How? Why can't you do it?"

She compressed her lips and moved closer to the bed. "Because I can't, you idiot. Don't you understand. However much rage I generate, nobody but you can see me." She grabbed his arm and Sam yelped in surprise at her ice cold touch. Gwen stopped, eyes wide. "What happened then?"

"You grabbed me."

"And you felt it." She pressed her finger into his arm but he felt nothing more than the soft caress of a spider web. "Can you feel that?"

"Not really. What does this mean?"

"Nothing," she said and got to her feet. "You need to go to her tomorrow and warn her."

"And say that you told me she was in danger?"

Gwen leaned in close, the earthy scent of her filling his nostrils and making him cough. "I don't care, just do it. I'll be watching you."

She faded into the dark.

From next door, Mum muttered, "Sam" and then shifted her position, the bed creaking under her.

Sam lay for a long time, staring at the bottom of the upper bunk, his mind a whirl.

Twelve

Gwen's face was inches from his, her fingers stroking his face. "Your eyes," she said, "let me see through your eyes."

Startled awake, Sam looked around the empty bedroom, faded sunlight bleaching the thin curtains. He let out a shaky breath and sat on the edge of the bed.

Last night's encounter must have been a bad dream, his mind conjuring up the horrific imagery as a way of coping with everything he'd gone through the past couple of days. It couldn't have been that the bump was more serious because, now he thought about it, his head didn't ache at all.

Standing up, the bruises caught his eye. Four finger-like impressions, they marred his upper arm where Gwen had grabbed him.

He felt sick. The marks weren't there last night which meant that, if they were real, he had to accept a ghost had told him Jess was in danger.

Stomach churning, he opened the bedroom door gently. Mum was in her room, the door closed. He rushed to the bathroom, had a quick shower and was back in his room, dried and getting dressed before she knocked on his door.

"Morning, Sammy, want some breakfast?"

"In a minute, Mum."

He tugged the sleeve of his t-shirt to try and cover the ever darkening bruises but that wasn't going to work. He went out.

Mum was on the step, smoking a cigarette, a cup of coffee beside her. She looked over her shoulder as he came through the door and her eyes looked dark, as if she'd had a sleepless night. Had Gwen been in her room too?

85

"You look tired."

"Wow." She raised her eyebrows. "You know how to make a woman of a certain age feel like a million dollars."

"I didn't mean that," he said quickly though he knew, really, he did. "You just look tired."

"Why quit while you're ahead?" Mum asked, offering him a wry smile. "I'm sure there's still some self-esteem you can take a pop at."

"Did you sleep well?"

"Like a log, I thought, but apparently I don't look like it."

"Do you feel okay?"

"Why wouldn't I?" She pulled at her cheek. "Do I really look that bad?"

"No, of course not. It's just, I heard you talking in your sleep and wondered if you'd had a bad dream." Such as, he wanted to say, a blonde woman creeping around your bedroom.

"I don't remember. Did I say anything exciting?"

"Not that I could make out, no."

"Probably a good thing." She took a drag. "So, have you got anything planned today?"

"Not really," he said and backed into the kitchen, keeping his arm out of sight. He put a couple of slices of bread into the toaster. "Want some?"

"No thanks, I'm going for a shower."

He willed the toaster to hurry up but it went slowly enough he thought he could do a quicker job using Mum's lighter. When it finally popped, she came into the caravan and went into her bedroom. He quickly spread the toast.

"I'm going to head out, see if I can find Polly."

"Okay." She padded barefoot from her bedroom, gave him a quick kiss on his forehead and went into the bathroom. Sam pulled on his cagoule and left, eating his toast as he went.

Visions of Ruin

Jogging up the reception steps, Sam quickly checked Gwen wasn't sitting on the chairs but the room was empty. A phone rang.

He walked to the counter. In the back room, a woman in a bright summer dress sat with her back to him, blonde hair loose to her shoulders. The phone still rang. When he pressed the bell it startled her and she jumped out of the chair, dropping a pen. Her crossword book fluttered to a close on the desk.

The woman came through the door with a friendly, "Morning, love." At least ten years older than Mum, so properly old, her make-up reminded him of Aunt Sally from Worzel Gummidge.

"Morning. I was wondering if I could speak to Jess?"

"She's not here at the moment. Are you a resident?""

""Yeah, I'm Sam Taylor from caravan 25."

She gave him a friendly smile that set off a heavy patina of lines around her eyes. "She was in earlier but booked the rest of the day off. Is there anything I can help you with?"

"Not really, I just wanted to tell her something. I'll catch her tomorrow."

"I'm sure you will," said the woman and she went back into the office.

As he turned away from the counter, Annie came through the door and waved. "Hey," she said, "how's our hero doing today?"

"I'm fine, thanks. Can I ask you a question?"

"Dunno, can you?" She put her hands on her hips and smiled. "What's up?"

"Do you know where Jess lives?"

She tilted her head. "You know she's got a boyfriend, don't you? And anyway, Polly's sweet on you."

The news shot a jolt through him. Was she right? He shook the idea away, needing to focus. "No, it's not like that, I have this thing and I need to drop it off for her."

"A thing?" Her smile broadened.

87

"Yes." He felt his cheeks colour. He was crap at thinking on his feet.

"Okay, I'll stop teasing you. Jess lives with her boyfriend on Carey Street. Do you know it?"

"Not at all."

"It's off the coast road, up near that weird old museum. There's a street map near the pier, you can check on there."

"Thanks, Annie, I appreciate it."

"It's number twenty four, I can't remember the flat but you'll see from the buzzers."

"Thanks."

"Not a problem." She went into the shop then stopped and turned to face him. "A little friendly advice," she said. "If I were you, I'd pay a bit of attention to Polly."

"Thanks," he said, feeling his cheeks colour some more as he pulled open the door.

"There you are," said Polly, startling him.

His cheeks felt like they were burning now. If he'd been living in a cartoon, there'd be a heat gauge attached to them, the dial whirling like a propeller.

She stood on the kerb, her fringe damp and starting to curl at the tips, her hood up. She scrunched her face into the light drizzle. "You doing much?"

"Not really." Should he tell her about last night or his mission today? Out of everyone he knew here, she was most likely to believe but there was a world of difference between a hanging victim from hundreds of years ago and the late wife of someone they vaguely knew.

"Are you blushing?"

"No."

"Are you that pleased to see me?"

"No," he said, without thinking, then stammered out, "wait, that didn't come out right."

"So what're you doing here?"

Annie's words rattled around his head. "I was looking for Jess," he said and knew, instantly, he'd made a mistake.

"Why?"

Shit. How did he get out of this? "Why what?"

Polly took a step forward. "Why were you looking for her?"

She clearly wasn't going to give up, which meant he would have to tell her. "Because something happened to me."

Her face creased in concern. "Bill wasn't waiting for you, was he?"

"No." The play park was empty so he gestured towards the swings. "Let's go in there."

She sat on the same swing as Jess had last night, but he sat next to her. "So, what happened?"

"I saw Gwen, Bill's first wife last night."

Polly went to say something but then her face creased into confusion. "That doesn't make sense."

"It will," he said, "but please don't laugh at me." He told her everything, as steadily and calmly as he could. She didn't laugh, instead listened intently and leaned towards him as if she didn't want to miss a word.

"That's incredible. But couldn't it have just been some horrible dream?"

"It could have been and that's what I hoped, until I found these." He pulled up the sleeve of his cagoule, the bruises even more livid now.

"Jesus, how did you get them?" Polly touched his arm and the contact felt wonderful.

"Gwen grabbed me. She seemed as surprised to make contact as I was."

"A ghost bruised you? Wow, that's fucking incredible, like a poltergeist or something."

"She wanted me to pay attention. She said Bill's a nasty piece of work and Jess is in danger."

"But I've known Jess for weeks now and she's never seemed nervous."

"Maybe she hides it because she's frightened. And what about her black eye, do you believe she walked into a door?"

"No, because she didn't, Sam. I saw her this morning and we were talking and, um…"

"What?"

"It was you, when you grabbed her. She felt you catch her face. I mean, you're a hero and everything and she didn't want to make you feel bad, so we agreed we wouldn't tell you."

"Fucking hell, I feel awful now."

"Whether you did it or not, there's clearly something about Bill that's wrong, especially if you've got the ghost of his first wife visiting you, to warn you."

"I know and since Jess is leaving town today, I need to find her and tell her to be careful."

"We should go then. Come on, I'll get Max to lend us a bike."

Thirteen

Carey Street was lined with Victorian three-storey terraces that looked dull and unloved. Trees, some as tall as the houses, dotted the pavements, slabs rippling around the roots.

Polly braked to a halt across the road and one house down from Number 32. "Do you know which flat?"

Sam shook his head as he looked up at the building. There were three chimneys set into the roof, which sagged under the weight. The top two floors had curtains drawn over the windows. The ground floor had a bay window, the glass sparkling and Sam could see a parrot strutting back and forth along a bar behind the central pane. "Maybe there's a buzzer or something by the door."

He walked briskly across the road and up the steps to the front door. A brass plate had three buttons set into it, with no markings against any of them.

"Doesn't help," said Polly.

An old man, stooped with age, pulled the door open and peered at them. His three-piece suit looked two sizes too big for him and his slippers had seen better days. What little of his hair remained was snowy white. "What do you kids want?"

"We were looking for someone," said Sam.

"Found him then, haven't you? Who are you?"

"I'm Sam Taylor, this is Polly Dutton."

"Pleased to meet you," she said.

The old man waved a hand at her. "I'm Mr Richardson, I live in the ground floor flat and I look after this house. Nobody here's got time for bob a job and I don't want me car washed."

"It's not you we're looking for," said Polly gently.

The old man stood as straight as he could, hands in the small of his back. "Charming. Bloody kids, today."

"We're looking for Bill Morgan, Mr Richardson," said Sam, "I was told he lives here."

"And who told you that?"

"Another friend."

Mr Richardson leaned close to him, squinting as if fixing Sam's face to memory. "Have lot of friends, do you?"

"Not really," said Sam, uncomfortable with the scrutiny. "I'm not trying to cause trouble, I'm just looking for Bill."

"I heard you the first time. Listen, I see everyone who comes in and out of this house."

"What if you're in the bathroom?" asked Polly.

"Then my parrot lets me know there's activity." He gestured towards the bird, watching them now from behind the glass. "Nobody's left the house this morning or come in, which means if Bill Morgan's here, he doesn't want to be disturbed by oiks like you."

"How do you know that?"

Mr Richardson chuckled. "Are you a bit simple, son? He doesn't want to be disturbed, up there with his girlfriend who's too bloody young for him."

"Jess," said Polly, "her name's Jess."

"He's much too old for her. I called him a cradle-snatcher the other day, he wasn't best pleased."

"I can imagine," muttered Polly.

"Will you let us in, so we can speak to him?"

"No. If I see him, I'll ask Bill if he wants to speak to you. How about that?"

"And if he says yes, how will you let us know?"

"Well," said Mr Richardson, giving them a gappy smile, "that's a bit of a problem, isn't it?" He shut the door.

Sam and Polly looked at one another. "Now what?" he asked.

"We wait and see if they come out."

It started to rain at a little after eleven, the patter of droplets on the canvas roof a mocking chorus.

"What if they don't come out at all?" Sam muttered.

"They have to if they're catching a train. Or maybe Mr Richardson will nip out and we can try and figure out a way to get in." Polly pushed against the pedals, stretching her legs. "I need to go to the loo."

Sam looked up and down the street. "Not much chance of that."

"I'll wander back towards the seafront and use one of the cafes." She slipped out of the bike and stretched, hands reaching for the sky before bending to touch her toes. He watched her move and thought about what Annie had said to him. Could she possibly have been right? "Did you want a can of something?" Polly asked, after she straightened up.

"A Coke please."

"Don't go anywhere," she said and walked away.

Sam blew out a breath and stared up at the house. It looked almost bland in the grey light, the rendered walls a pale sickly colour. Which of them was Bill's? Had he lived there before, with Gwen? Could that be where he'd first thought about murdering her?

"What are you doing here?"

Startled, Sam grabbed the handlebar to stop himself falling out the bike. Gwen sat in Polly's seat. "Sorry," she said with a smile that didn't look at all amused. "Did I scare you?"

He glanced over his shoulder, hoping to see Polly coming back, but nobody was about. "Of course you bloody did." He edged sideways, not wanting to sit too close.

"That's unkind," she said. "And you never answered me, about why you're here."

"I'm doing what you said, making sure Jess is okay."

"I never told you to come."

"How else was I supposed to do it? She's leaving today."

Gwen looked surprised. "What do you mean?"

"They're leaving town. I came so I could try and warn her but the old man on the ground floor wouldn't let us in."

"Ah, old George the guard dog. He must have some stories to tell, with what he's heard in his time."

Sam nodded, willing Polly to come back. Seeing Gwen in his bedroom had been terrifying enough but now, in the daylight, it seemed worse. Her skin looked waxy, stretched too tight over the bone structure of her face and neck. Worse, as she moved, there was some kind of stutter in his vision – like she was a video image where the tracking needed to be adjusted, a lenticular picture with a glitch.

"Did your mum never tell you it's rude to stare?"

"I can't help it."

"No," she said and gave him a dead smile, "and I forgive you because you helped me discover something last night."

"What?"

She reached for him and he shied away. "Don't hurt my feelings, Sam." Her fingertips brushed the back of his hand, her skin cold and hard. A chill seeped into his skin, making his veins ache and pain sparked at his temples, throbbing across his forehead.

"It hurts," he said.

"Hush." She put her hand over his and the cold got worse, the way ice does if you hold it too long. The chill seeped into his fingers and, all of a sudden, he felt tired to his bones. Maybe the lack of sleep last night was getting to him, maybe Gwen wasn't even here, maybe he was already asleep and this was just the start of a nightmare.

"Hey, sleepyhead."

Polly's voice seemed a long way away and it took Sam a moment or two to realise he'd nodded off. His arm ached slightly and he had a crick in his neck, where his head had lolled back. He tried to wipe his mouth as surreptitiously as he could, just in case he'd drooled. "Sorry."

"Don't worry, you had a busy night. I don't think I'd have slept much either." She handed him a can of Coke. Her hair was damp, her eyes bright. The rain had stopped, by the sound of it.

"Thanks." He popped the ring pull and dropped it into the can. "I had the weirdest dream."

"About what?"

"That Gwen was here."

Polly laughed. "You have such an imagination." She looked around anyway, as if checking the ghost woman wasn't loitering nearby. "Did she say anything?"

"She wondered why I was here and that she'd learned something from me last night."

"Weird. And how about the old man, did he come out while you were awake?"

"No." Sam's fingers felt slightly numb, his arm heavy as if he'd slept on it funny and he looked at the back of his hand. "Oh shit." There was a mark, like the start of a bruise and the veins, radiating out of the discoloration, were dark. The nail on his little finger looked like it had a blood bruise under it.

"Bloody hell, when did that happen?"

"It wasn't there before you left, was it?" He tried to think but all he could remember was his dream, of Gwen touching the back of his hand and saying he'd taught her something.

"No, I don't think so. It looks like you bashed it on something."

Had she really touched him? "Maybe I did."

"Well be careful, you already look pale, like you're coming down with something." She touched the back of his hand, her fingertips warm and soft.

He flexed his fingers, feeling slowly returning with painful pins and needles.

Polly settled into her seat and opened her can of Quatro. They sat quietly for almost fifteen minutes, occasionally glancing towards the house.

"He's coming out," she said, ducking low.

Sam leaned down, peering over her head. Mr Richardson adjusted his trilby and closed the front door, then tapped on his window and waited until the parrot walked towards him. With a smile, he came down the steps, surveyed the street, then walked off towards the seafront.

"Come on," said Polly, "let's go."

They rushed across the road, raindrops still being shed from the trees that formed a canopy above them. Sam followed Polly up the steps to the doors. The parrot squawked loudly enough for them to hear, flapping its wings and tapping its beak on the glass. It didn't seem at all happy.

"So what's the plan?" Polly asked.

"I thought you had one."

"Not really," she said and pressed all three buttons at once. The sounds of chimes and buzzers drifted through the door. She pressed them again.

"What?" came a crackly voice.

"I have a parcel for Mr Richardson," she said.

"Leave it by the door, the old codger'll find it."

"But it's cardboard, it'll go all funny in the rain."

"Jesus," said the voice and a buzzer sounded, loud enough to make her jump. "Push the door."

"Thanks."

The hall was narrow and dark, with vinyl tiles and a matt to wipe your feet. Mr Richardson's front door, with a sticker reading "flat 1" above the door handle, was on the right. A small side table stood across from it, holding a pile of post and a pot plant that looked very dead. Polly picked up the envelopes and sifted through them.

"Flat 2," she said. "Any idea what you're going to say?"

"Nope."

The stairs were narrow, the carpet loose in places. Pictures had hung over the banister once but they were long gone, leaving only patches of brighter wallpaper. There was another pot plant on the first landing, this one in better health, next to the door of Bill's flat. The stairs went up further, the light looking even gloomier up there.

Sam looked at Polly and bit his lip. She looked at him. Now they were here, he wasn't quite sure what to do next. How could he tell Jess she was in danger from the boyfriend who, more than likely, was in the same room as her?

"Are you going to knock?" Polly whispered.

"I don't know what to say."

Polly tilted her head as she considered. "Make it up as you go along," she said and knocked.

"Who's there?" Bill called a moment or two later.

Sam looked at Polly, raised his eyebrows.

"Brownies," she said, "I'm selling biscuits."

"Don't want any," Bill called back. "Did George let you in?"

"My granddad is a friend of his." She gave Sam a weak smile and stuck up her thumb. "He said it'd be okay."

There was a murmur of conversation before Bill said "hold on." A security chain was moved, locks undone. The door opened and Sam stepped to one side, so he wouldn't be seen.

"Aren't you a bit old to be a Brownie?" Bill asked.

"Is that you, Polly?"

"Sorry we had to lie, Jess, but we needed to speak to you." Polly pulled Sam into view.

"You!" Bill said, his voice loud and full of edges.

Sam tried to ignore him. "I need to speak to you, Jess."

"She's not interested in speaking to you," insisted Bill and tried to shut the door.

Sam put his foot down, the door bouncing off the toe of his trainers. "Please, Jess."

She touched Bill's shoulder. "Let him talk."

"Why?" Bill asked, turning on her, "So he can lie like he did before? The kid scared the shit out of you with all that vision bollocks."

"And you scared the shit out of him, let him talk."

"He's not fucking coming in."

"I don't want to," said Sam, "I can say it all out here."

"Go on then," taunted Bill.

Sam took a deep breath and let it out slowly. The man terrified him but so did the idea of seeing Gwen again. He looked up, half expecting to see her in the shadows of the next landing.

"Sam?" Jess said, following his gaze up the stairs.

He only had a matter of moments before Bill tried again to shut him up. "You're in danger." His heart hammered loud enough he thought everyone would hear it. "You mustn't go to the train station."

Bill glared at Jess. "You told him?"

"I had to. He's not a bad kid, Bill."

"What did you do to your arm?" Polly asked.

Jess looked at her elbow, pulling the sleeve of her t-shirt down. "Nothing."

"Is that a bruise?" Polly demanded.

Sam tried to see but Bill stepped in front of him.

"You're a real big man, aren't you?" Polly's voice rose, along with the colour in her cheeks. "Do you enjoy knocking women and teenagers about?"

"I didn't fucking hit Jess, I've never fucking hit Jess."

Jess held his arm and Sam saw the dark bruises just above her elbow and instantly recognised them. "No, I don't think you did."

"What?"

Sam pulled up his cagoule sleeve. His bruises were exactly the same as Jess'.

"Shit," muttered Polly.

"How did you get them?" Jess asked.

Sam turned his hand over. The bruise on the back of it had deepened in colour and now most of his little finger was bruised too.

"Ow," said Polly, "that looks painful."

"That wasn't me," Bill said, "I didn't touch you."

"It was Gwen," Sam said.

Bill roared and slapped the door with both hands, slamming it fully open and into the wall. He stalked back into the flat, brushing past Jess who stared at Sam's hand like it was some exotic jewel she'd never seen before.

"How did that happen, Sam?"

"Gwen," he said. "I saw her last night."

Jess shook her head, eyes wide with terror. "That can't be, Sam."

"I know, I don't understand it any more than you do. But she was in my room. I thought I was dreaming but then I found these."

Bill came back to the door. "You're a liar."

"No," Sam said, "I'm not. I saw her again this morning, outside here, wearing a white t-shirt and red jeans."

Bill visibly blanched. "White t-shirt and red jeans?" he asked.

Jess looked into the flat, as if frightened.

"You told me it was a dream," said Polly.

"She touched the back of my hand."

"Did you feel washed out this morning?" Jess asked quietly. Everyone looked at her. "I woke up feeling like I hadn't slept in weeks."

"Not this morning, but just now, outside, yes."

"I woke him up," said Polly. "He looked terrible."

"What the fuck is going on?" Jess asked.

"It's that bloody woman," said Bill. "Even now, even after all this, I can't get away from her."

"What do you mean?" Polly said.

Bill ignored her and turned to Jess. "I told you we needed to get away."

"What's going on," she said, "you're frightening me."

He put a hand on her shoulder then turned to Sam and Polly. "Thank you," he said, "but now kindly fuck off." He slammed the door shut and they heard raised voices through the wood. Sam knocked on the door again but the voices moved away.

"What do we do now?" Polly asked.

"We have to stop them going to the train station," said Sam.

Fourteen

"You said it was a dream," Polly said, clearly hurt. "You didn't tell me she'd caused that bruise and I thought you knew you could trust me."

Sam pulled the front door shut behind him and Mr Richardson's parrot went spare, flapping its wings and hitting the glass. Polly crossed the road and he traipsed behind her, feeling like a complete shit.

"I do trust you."

She slid into her side of the bike and folded her arms, staring down the street.

"I'm sorry," he said and climbed onto his seat.

"You're a shit."

"I know, I just…" He took a deep breath and let it out slowly. "I do trust you, I promise. You believed me, when I said I'd seen her last night and so there's no reason to think you wouldn't believe me again, but it was in the street, in daylight and I was asleep. And how could she do this to me, or to Jess? She's a ghost."

"But you said it yourself, she's angry with Bill. Maybe she can focus that anger somehow? She hurt you the first time she touched you last night but the second time, you said it felt like a spiders web or whatever." She threw up her hands. "I don't know what I'm saying. We need Roy's wife here, she'd be able to explain it all."

"Well, unless I start seeing her as well, that's not going to happen is it?"

Polly gave him a look then leaned back. Sam watched her for a moment, waiting for her to speak, not sure if she was waiting for him to say anything or not. The silence pressed into him, horribly uncomfortable. Why didn't she say something?

Mr Richardson came back carrying a Co-op plastic bag. At the bottom of the steps he looked up and down the street, his gaze sweeping over their bike without apparently seeing them. As he fished his keys from his pocket, he tapped the window and the parrot regarded him for a moment then walked away.

"That parrot's pissed off Mr Richardson wasn't there to stop us," Sam said.

Polly glanced at him with the hint of a smile. "I wonder if he'll tell him."

"If Mr Richardson comes chasing out after us, we'll know, won't we?"

Polly laughed and the atmosphere in the bike lifted, much to Sam's relief.

"You know," she said, "I did read something in that book Pam helped write, the one Roy showed us and it's making me think."

"What did it say?"

"It was about ghosts being corporeal."

"What the hell does that mean?"

"It means a body, like flesh and bone, what a ghost isn't. They're lost souls that can't interact with anything because they don't exist in this realm."

She looked as though she expected him to follow her train of thought but he didn't. He shrugged.

"Think about it, most people see ghosts as shadows or transparent beings, like that person you saw hanging in the light. Sometimes, though, if the ghost is driven by love or rage or a desire to communicate, they can make a connection and cross between our realm and theirs. That's what Pam claims, in any case. They're the weird things you see in photographs, a cold sensation and noises that shouldn't happen. If the ghost realises this, the research reckons they can deepen that connection and increase their presence."

"You mean, make themselves corporeal?"

"Precisely. That focus might mean their voices get picked up by tape recorders or play notes on an instrument, or throw books around."

"Like a poltergeist?"

"Yes, which can be bloody dangerous. If they're angry, they're going to wreck something, aren't they? A few years ago there was a case in London where these two girls heard knocking sounds and chairs wobbled and turned over and toys got thrown around. Their mum had to call the police, in the end."

"So if everyone thought you'd committed suicide but you hadn't and your husband not only got away with it but went off with someone much younger, you wouldn't be happy?"

"It'd make *me* bloody angry," she said. "And what if you'd been trying to communicate that your husband killed you but nobody could see or hear you? Then a random teenager gets bonked on the head and, for some reason, is able to see things the rest of us can't."

"You make me sound like a freak."

She held up her hands. "I'm just saying. Until you got into that fight, you'd never had a vision or seen a ghost before, had you? And Gwen figures this out because she's watching her husband, waiting for her chance and suddenly realises you can see her. It wouldn't take much to find you or perhaps, if you can see ghosts, it's like you're carrying a big neon arrow for them."

If Polly was on the right track, how many other ghosts had he seen here so far? "Did you see a sailor in the museum?"

"I didn't see anyone other than you and Roy."

"I saw a sailor, in full naval dress, walk by us in the foyer and go upstairs."

"Fucking hell, Sam, that's bloody scary because you heard what Roy said about his son." She shivered and rubbed her arms. "But if Gwen knows you can see her, why wouldn't she try and get you to help?"

"So what's with the grabbing and the bruises? Why hurt me and Jess?"

Polly opened her mouth as if she was going to say something and then snapped it shut, looking towards the house. Sam watched, waiting for her to say whatever was on her mind. When she didn't, he tapped her shoulder.

"What?" he asked.

"No," she said, without looking at him, "it's stupid."

"With what we're talking about, how can anything be stupid now?"

"Okay, this is just a theory." She faced him. "When I found you asleep, you looked knackered. Jess said she felt washed out. What if Gwen isn't just running on anger and has figured out a way to drain energy from you to give herself corporeality."

"That's ridiculous."

"I told you it was." She held his hand, turned it over in hers. The bruise was livid, his little finger nail now completely black. "What if I'm at least half right though? What if she can make herself more real in this world by taking some kind of essence from you and Jess?"

"But why would she do that?"

"She's angry, maybe she wants to get her own back."

"What if she's here now, waiting for another chance to get more energy?"

They both quickly twisted around in their seats, but Sam couldn't see Gwen anywhere.

"I've wanted to see a ghost forever," said Polly, "but now that it might happen, I'm really not sure it's such a good idea."

Fifteen

The clouds darkened as the day wore on, threatening rain that never actually came.

Polly directed Sam to the café so he could use the loo, then bought them lunch from the same place, two sausage rolls in a paper bag that was slick with grease stains by the time she got back to the bike. She only had enough money for one can of Coke and they shared it.

She talked a lot and he was happy to listen, anything to keep his mind off the thought of seeing Gwen again. He kept checking Bill's window, wondering what they were doing and if he'd somehow misunderstood when they were leaving. In the end, he said as much to Polly.

"Last train'll be about nine o'clock, then we'll head back," she said. "There's no way I'm staying overnight on this thing."

Close to tea-time, their stomachs rumbling, Polly noticed movement.

Bill looked out the front door and the parrot danced in the window. A car turned into the street from the seafront and Sam shifted in his seat so he could see it.

"It's a black cab."

"They're off then," Polly said. "We need to get a move on, they'll be faster than us."

"Are you sure we shouldn't wait, to make sure they get in it?"

The cab stopped outside number 24, its engine idling noisily. The driver honked the horn.

"It's them," she said. "Come on."

Polly steered with purpose, urging him to pedal faster, not bothering to brake at junctions. Several cars sounded their horns and she raised a hand to each driver, though Sam didn't think it placated them much.

The taxi went by them on one street and he turned his head away, just in case Bill or Jess looked out of the window.

By the time they reached the railway station he was knackered, his legs aching and lungs burning. The taxi idled outside the main door, Bill pulling a large suitcase out of the boot. Jess was carrying a rucksack that looked almost too heavy for her.

The Victorian brown brick building had a slate roof heavily repaired in a hodge-podge of dark coloured tiles. Polly steered them into an unpaved car park, the bike bouncing through pot holes and stopped it against a wooden fence that leaned at a drunken angle.

They slipped out and ducked down, peering over the top of the fence as Bill and Jess went through an archway and out of sight. As the cab pulled away, Polly tapped Sam on the shoulder and they ran down to the archway, through which an alley led to the platform. Sam stopped at the corner and peered around. He couldn't see Bill or Jess.

The platform was shielded by six arches of translucent sheeting, held up by ornately decorated ironwork columns. A yellow bench stood beside the door to the ticket office. Across two sets of tracks was another platform, with a waiting room, shielded by a similar canopy. To his right, an iron footbridge enclosed by sheet metal parapets spanned the rails. Both platforms were empty.

"They're not here," he said.

Polly leaned against his shoulder and peered around. "If they're going over the bridge, we should see them in a minute."

When Bill appeared at the top of the stairs, Polly grabbed Sam's hand and pulled him onto the platform. They raced to the stairs and took them two at a time, their footsteps too loud in Sam's ears. Surely, with all this racket, Bill would hear them?

They crossed the bridge and walked slowly down the other staircase. Pain flared in Sam's temples and got worse with every step, like someone hitting him with a wooden spoon.

Bill and Jess stood in front of the waiting room door. She'd leaned her rucksack against the wall and he had the suitcase between his feet.

He almost did a double take when he spotted Sam, his face clouding and forehead creasing. "What're you bastards doing here?"

Jess jumped and Sam thought he saw sadness in her expression. She put a hand on Bill's chest. "Calm down."

"*Calm down?* They're bloody chasing after us!"

Sam's heart raced, the pain in his head getting worse. His stomach rolled and he thought, for one terrible moment, he was going to throw up. "I've come to help you," he said, wincing at how weak he sounded.

Bill shook his head disgustedly. "If you've come to see me throw Jess under a train, you're going to be horribly disappointed." He didn't sound so angry now, more resigned.

"I just told her what I saw."

Bill took Jess' hand. "You had a fucking vision, you idiot. The seaside's full of people who'll tell your fortune for a few quid and they're all a con, just like you. I don't know what your fucking angle is, but Jess is not in danger."

"That's not how it looks to us," Polly said.

"Oh is that right, love?" Bill asked. "And you know I'm dangerous, do you?"

"I believe Sam," she said.

"And what if I don't? What happens then?"

"Jess," said Sam, "I've never experienced anything like this before but I know what I saw."

"What you think you saw," Bill clarified. "If you were so worried, you'd have told the police. But you can't, because you'd have to tell them you talked to my late wife."

It sounded ridiculous because it was ridiculous but Sam couldn't leave it now. "You know they wouldn't believe me but it doesn't change what I saw."

Bill took a step towards him, Jess pulling his arm. Sam stood his ground. "You didn't see anything, you stupid kid. You're just buying into all the lies she told."

"What lies?" Polly asked.

"That everything was to do with me, that I was the bully and the abuser."

"All you've done since I've known you is shout and throw your weight around," said Polly.

Bill glanced at her, lips pursed, then back at Sam. "Keep your girlfriend under control, mate, she's saying things you're going to end up paying for."

"I'm not his girlfriend," Polly said, pointedly, "and threatening me just makes you sound even more of a bully."

"Bill, come on," said Jess, trying to pull him back. "It's not worth it, we'll be gone soon."

"But you can't," said Sam, "something's going to happen." The hairs on his arms stood on end, as if he'd just touched something filled with static.

"What do you get out of this, you little twat? You don't know me and you certainly didn't know Gwen." He took several deep breaths and looked up at the sky before fixing his full attention on Sam. "She lied right from the beginning but people believed her because why wouldn't they? It's much easier to believe it's the husband doing all the hurting, isn't it?"

The electrical charge Sam felt in the air slid down his back, making his muscles twitch.

"Look at this," Bill said and stepped forward suddenly. Sam held his ground but Bill didn't raise his fists. Instead, he leaned forward slightly, pulling on the neckline of his shirt to expose his throat and clavicles. "Look."

Sam found it hard to focus, his head filling with a noise like the hiss of a punctured tyre. "At what?"

"This," said Bill. Dark chest hair stopped just below the line of what looked like a seashell necklace.

Sam leaned in, his head now singing with pain and realised he'd made a mistake. They weren't shells on a necklace, they were burn marks on Bill's skin.

"She did the first one when we were lying in bed. I screamed and she just laughed, can you imagine that? Told me not to be a baby, that she'd only done it because she wondered what it'd look like."

Aware that Polly was leaning forward, trying to see for herself, Sam said, "how?"

"A cigarette," said Bill. He unbuttoned a cuff and pushed the sleeve sharply up his arm. A meandering trail of similar burn marks led from a few inches above his wrist to his elbow. Polly gasped.

"She burned you?" she asked.

"Uh huh, she did everything she could think of, even broke my finger once. I couldn't wait to get away. When she died, people latched onto the fact I didn't get upset but I was the happiest I'd ever been."

"She told me you killed her."

"Of course she fucking did, what else is she going to say?"

The tannoy squawked into life and the announcer said the next train wouldn't be stopping in the station and passengers should move away from the edge.

The light above the waiting room door flickered into life and the hissing Sam could hear grew louder. He looked across the platform and saw Gwen standing beside the yellow bench. The light flickered again and a train horn sounded.

"Don't listen to him," Gwen said, her voice a whisper in his ear. "He's nothing but a liar."

Jess screamed. When Sam glanced at her, he wasn't surprised to see her staring with wide eyes at the opposite platform.

"What?" Bill demanded. "What is it?"

"I can see something, a shape in a shadow."

The pain in Sam's temples spiked and his head suddenly felt too heavy for his neck. The static charged drained and he felt faint. Was that what she'd been doing, draining his energy so she could appear to Jess?

"What's going on?" Bill demanded, his voice cracking with doubt. He was looking at the platform, despair etched into his expression.

"She can see something of me," said Gwen, now beside Sam, her voice a breath against his neck. "But I'm not strong enough."

She grabbed his hand. The burn was instantaneous and he tried to jerk free of her grasp. Both Bill and Polly reached for him.

"Are you getting a shock or something?" Polly asked.

"No, no, *no!*" said Jess.

Sam managed to shake Gwen off and she backed away from him. "You've given me enough for what I need," she said, smiling widely.

The train horn boomed and the tannoy clicked on, but nobody spoke. The light above the waiting room door glowed too brightly and then the bulb popped.

Polly held his arm, concern creasing her face. "What happened, Sam? Are you okay?" She looked at him intently. "You look worse now than you did before."

He held up his right hand, the bruise already darkening the skin. "She's here."

"Gwen?" said Bill. "That's impossible."

"It's not," said Sam. "This is what I saw. The train isn't going to stop, we have to…" Jess screamed, cutting him off.

She was moving backwards, towards the tracks, leaning forward at the waist as she reached for them. Gwen pulled her but the others couldn't see that, just an impossible nightmarish vision. Polly screamed, adding to the confusion.

Sam reached for Jess. Bill didn't move. He shook the man's arm but Bill only stared, his expression vacant as logic was sucked out of his world. He kicked Bill hard in the shins and that got his attention.

"Grab Jess," Sam said and held her left hand, tugging back as hard as he could. She still moved and Gwen glared at him.

"Don't try to help," she said. "Bill's mine, this whore doesn't deserve him."

"Bill," Sam shouted, trying to ignore the angry ghost, "grab her other arm."

Bill did but it wasn't enough. Polly tried to help, pulling Sam's other hand but his trainers slipped across the platform as Jess slid ever closer to the rails.

The train horn sounded, loud enough he felt it in his bones.

"Get her away from the edge!" Polly shouted.

Bill leaned back and the pressure showed in Jess' face, her lips tight against gritted teeth. Gwen moved steadily, as if she felt no resistance.

The air carried the vibration of the train.

Sam, straining so hard he heard popping in his ears, tried to think of a way to counter Gwen. He daren't let go of Jess, not with the train this close. Every blink showed him how she was in the vision, grasping for him as she fell towards the tracks, the train vaporising her seconds later.

Bill stumbled and lost his grip on Jess' wrist. With Sam still pulling her, she twisted, slipping out of Gwen's grasp too.

The apparition screamed "no!"

The train whistle blew.

Bill pitched forward, momentum pushing him towards the track.

Jess fell into Sam and he embraced her tightly, falling back against the waiting room wall.

Bill was too close to the edge of the platform. Gwen reached for him but Sam could see through her now, whatever strength she'd had draining away. She caught his hand and Bill cried out, tipping over the edge.

The engine roared into the station, horn blasting the air.

Gwen reached for Bill one last time and then he was gone.

The police arrived quickly.

Sam and Jess were spoken to individually, her in the station master's office, him in the waiting room. Jess was sedated and taken away in an ambulance and nobody would tell Sam or Polly how she was.

The station master, hearing the shouts, was on the other platform as Bill fell onto the tracks and saw, clearly, that the others were nowhere near him. Sam also overheard the station master tell the officer in charge he'd seen some kind of shape, a weird shadow, reaching for the dead man moments before he fell.

As Sam was led from the waiting room, he looked along the track. The train had stopped just outside the station, its passengers shepherded off into buses which took them down to Great Yarmouth station to continue their journey.

"Nasty business," said the policeman escorting Sam. "I loved trains as a lad and wanted to be in the Transport Police until I realised I'd be looking at suicides all the time."

"He didn't commit suicide."

"So you said but that's what we usually call it when people dive in front of a train. Bugger of a thing to do, really. Think of the poor driver. And the poor sod who's got to collect up all the body parts." He jutted his chin at the officers in white paper suits who worked their way steadily along the track.

Sam looked across at the other platform and, for a moment, his headache flared again, beating against his temples.

Bill stood by the yellow bench, looking scared. Gwen, beside him, held Bill's arm and hand tightly. She looked at Sam, put her index finger to her lips and shook her head.

Behind her, a small crowd had gathered. As she pulled Bill away and he mouthed a silent scream to Sam, the crowd parted to let them through. Gwen spoke to a tall man in a business suit and he locked eyes with Sam and tipped him a wink.

Startled, Sam could only stare back.

The tall man pointed at Sam and the rest of the crowd looked his way.

"He can see us," he heard a multitude of voices say. "That boy can see us."

About the Author

Mark West lives in Northamptonshire with his wife Alison and their son Matthew. Since discovering the small press in 1998 he has published over eighty short stories, two novels, a novelette, a chapbook, two collections and six novellas in the horror genre and is about to have a mainstream thriller published.

Away from writing, he enjoys reading, walking and watching films. He can be contacted through his website at www.markwest.org.uk or on Twitter as @MarkEWest

Author's Acknowledgements:

Thanks to: Alison; Mum & Dad; Sarah, Chris and my wonderful bookworm nieces Lucy & Milly, who were keen to hear what was happening in my ghost story; Nick, who was there in 1985 with me; Ian Whates for asking me to write this and also for running the best writing group there is; David & Pippa for the Friday Night Walks and all those plotting sessions that put all this together, and Dude, who's 16 and makes me proud with everything he does (even listening patiently on our walks across the fields as I work through ideas).

CPSIA information can be obtained
at www.ICGtesting.com
Printed in the USA
LVHW011041300322
714730LV00010B/648